RUSSELL WAGNER WAS HAVING A HARD TIME ON PRISON HILL.

Slocum realized that there was no time to plan an elaborate break-out. Every day counted. He sighed.

It was quiet in the saloon now. Slocum cradled his glass in his palms. He could hear the heavy, calm tick-tock of the grandfather clock behind the bar.

Slocum knew there was only one answer. He had to get into Yuma, find Russell Wagner, and bring him out.

And the only way to get into Yuma was to commit a felony...

OTHER BOOKS BY JAKE LOGAN

JAKE LOGAN

JAILBREAK
MOON

BERKLEY BOOKS, NEW YORK

JAILBREAK MOON

A Berkley Book / published by arrangement with
the author

PRINTING HISTORY
Berkley edition / November 1985

ISBN: 0-425-08189-3

A BERKLEY BOOK® TM 757,375
Berkley Books are published by The Berkley Publishing Group,
200 Madison Avenue, New York, N.Y. 10016.
The name "BERKLEY" and the stylized "B" with design are trademarks
belonging to Berkley Publishing Corporation.

PRINTED IN THE UNITED STATES OF AMERICA

JAILBREAK
MOON

1

Henry Wagner said harshly, "Let's get to the point, Slocum. My son made a stupid mistake. He's paying for it at the Territorial Prison." His self-control was dangerously near the edge.

Slocum could not blame the man. The Territorial Prison at Yuma was a hell-hole set at a strategic point—the confluence of the Gila and Colorado Rivers. Yuma was a way station on the road to California. Its heat and mosquitoes were notorious throughout Arizona. The prison was surrounded by desert. Its cells were blasted from a granite bluff; men had escaped from it, but the lack of water and the generous bounty given to the Indians who captured escapees were very effective barriers. Experienced criminals considered it the worst—and most secure—prison in the United States.

Slocum nodded sympathetically. He could not figure out why Wagner, a rich cattleman whose vast herds roamed the grasslands under the Mogollon Rim, had contacted him.

"That goddamn prison is a killer," Wagner said bitterly. He had been holding a cigar in his right hand. Now he bit the end off angrily and fumbled for a match. His hand trembled. The heat, the flies, and the mosquitoes of the fever-ridden delta of the Colorado River killed off many prisoners as surely as the hangman's noose.

Wagner finally succeeded in lighting his cigar. He pulled in a long inhale, let it out, and said, somewhat more under control, "Russell's not a bad boy." His voice had become firm and commanding, its usual tone. He was a big, burly man of fifty-five with a full head of grey hair. He wore a white linen suit and his forty-dollar sombrero lay on the table next to Slocum's bottle of beer. He wore handmade boots that must have cost three months' wages for one of his riders.

Slocum said nothing, but he looked sympathetically at the anguish of Russell Wagner's father. Still, Slocum thought that "boy" was not quite the right word to describe Wagner's son. Russell was not a boy. He was a man of twenty-six. He had been arrested seven times since he was eighteen. Six times the charge was disorderly conduct: riding his horse into a saloon, discharging a weapon inside city limits, breaking windows. All these were disposed of with a twenty-five- or fifty-dollar fine, which his father paid, contenting himself with the thought that these actions were due simply to the exuberance of youth.

Then one evening, at the Silver Queen Saloon in Tucson, Russell shot and killed a tinhorn gambler he had accused of cheating at faro. Witnesses said that the gambler had not only not drawn his gun, he had not even made a move toward it. Moreover, Russell had fired when the gambler had turned his back.

The district attorney asked the grand jury for an indictment of murder in the second degree. The grand jury was composed of wealthy citizens, many of whom liked and respected Henry Wagner. They rebuffed the hard-working D.A. and voted to lower the charges to manslaughter.

The disgruntled D.A. tried the case and won a conviction on the manslaughter charge.

"When was sentencing?" Slocum asked. He watched an attractive woman walk across the lobby. As she prepared to climb the stairs to the second floor, she pulled up her long black skirt. She was wearing high-heeled high-buttoned black shoes with a heavy gloss on them. Slocum fantasized her naked save for her shoes. The thought caused an electric current to run through his groin. He had just ridden into Tucson after a wild goose chase for Maximilian's Treasure down in Mexico. He had not found it, and he was tired, broke, and exhausted.

"Beg your pardon," he said. "I missed that."

Henry Wagner lit an expensive cigar and glowered at him. He was used to deferential behavior from everyone he met, from the governor of the territory on down. But this tall, hard-bitten man with the tanned face, cold green eyes, and hard, calloused hands covered with rope burns and barbed-wire scars was not being deferential. Indeed, to Wagner it seemed as if Slocum didn't give a goddamn about anything. He was polite, yes. Deferential, no.

Wagner repeated what he had just said. "Sentencing was a month ago. Judge McClean is a friend of mine. Because of extenuating circumstances—" Here Wagner permitted himself a thin smile—"he gave my boy five years. He could have given him fifteen."

The smile told Slocum that extenuating circumstances probably meant a quiet cash transaction. A man like Henry

Wagner had not clawed his way to the top without using every weapon he could lay his hands on.

"With good behavior he should be out in three years," Slocum said as he drained his glass. It was hot outside, and he had not had a cold drink for months.

"You don't know my boy," Wagner said. He rolled his cigar between his fingers as he stared at the tiled floor. "He never could control his temper. I hear there's a lot of hardcases in Yuma. He might push one of them a little too far. Or he might break down and try to go over the wall. I've heard stories about men who went crazy in there. They start to climb the wall in broad daylight and the guards in the tower blow them apart with that Gatling gun they have up there."

Slocum's face showed his sympathy. Wagner noticed his expression.

"I don't want your goddamn sympathy," Wagner coldly said. "What I want is for you to get into Yuma prison and take him out with you."

Any other time Slocum would have stood up at once, bowed politely, as he had been taught to do to older men, expressed his regrets, and withdrawn.

But right now all that Slocum owned in the world were the clothes he was wearing, a pair of run-down boots which needed new soles and heels, a .44 with only seven cartridges in his gunbelt, and a battered Winchester with three cartridges. He had used the others in his ride to the border. His horse was a thin bay with its ribs sticking out like a xylophone. The horse was now enjoying a feast of oats at Logan's Livery Stable. Logan trusted Slocum to pay him whenever he could.

Mexico was a bad country to try to extract a fortune from; Slocum was very lucky to have made it in one piece to the border. In his saddlebag were five silver dollars, an extra shirt that needed laundering, a straight razor, and a bar of harsh laundry soap which served to wash and launder. He had left his battered skillet and coffee pot in a hurried dawn departure from his camp at the Rio Yaqui.

But getting someone out of Yuma Territorial Prison would be even harder. There was no chance of success.

He shook his head with regret and stood up.

"Mr Wagner—" he began.

Wagner said, "Thirty thousand and all expenses."

With thirty thousand a man could stock a ranch. Not only that, he could make a down payment on a good one where the weather was always fine—say, central California. No cattle-killing blizzards, no drought such as was common in the Texas Panhandle. Don Ramon Escobar was willing to sell such a spread, near the San Joaquin. But he wanted twenty thousand dollars in gold as a down payment.

Now it could be in his grasp.

Still, Yuma was just too hard a nut to crack. Slocum started to shake his head.

Wagner took out his wallet. He took out five hundred dollars in new fifties. "Here's five hundred, Mr. Slocum," he said. "Just to look over the situation. If you decide against it, the five hundred is yours."

Slocum considered. That was an offer he could live with.

"Not saying I'll go through with it," Slocum said slowly, "but if I say no, the five hundred is mine and we're quits?"

"We're quits," Wagner said. He lit another cigar. He had himself under control, but Slocum could see that his eyes were pleading for help. "But from what I've heard people say who know you, you'd prefer to earn that twenty-nine thousand, five hundred."

Slocum said nothing. He held out his hand. Wagner let

out a sigh of relief and handed Slocum the five hundred dollars.

Slocum had no particular fondness for the bay eating his oats at Logan's. He had lifted it from a *hacienda* northwest of Magdalena in Chihuahua, and had ridden it hard. Logan offered Slocum a hundred and fifty for it. It was worth more, but Slocum didn't want a horse eating expensive oats while he studied the situation at Yuma, over two hundred miles to the west. Logan said he could store his saddle and Winchester at his tack room, no charge.

He took the Butterfield stage the next day. It rattled and banged across the southwestern part of Arizona Territory along the gentle curving course of the Gila. The trip took three hard days. At the food stops there were beans, tortillas, and tough beefsteaks, slapped on the rough wooden tables by sullen, sweating waiters. Burned-out wagons littered the roadside where Apache renegades from San Carlos had struck. The driver and the guard both carried shotguns.

At Yuma he got off as soon as the stage crossed on the ferry to the west bank of the Colorado River. Yuma clung to the western shore where the river made a sharp right curve on its way to its mouth at the Gulf of California. It sat grimly with its adobe buildings baking in the fierce heat.

He found a saloon on Gila Street, a dusty road that paralleled the muddy brown river. The saloon was named Hell's Half Acre. Slocum walked in and ordered bourbon. He slung his saddlebags across a nearby table and leaned on the bar.

The bartender said idly, "Stranger in these parts?"

"Gettin' tired of winters in the Sierra," Slocum said. "Headin' south to Mexico. Mebbe git a job in some *hacienda* where they need a top hand. Show 'em a thing or two 'bout cowboyin'! Yessir!"

A little boasting never failed to provoke responses. Too quiet a presence, just hanging around listening and keeping one's mouth shut could provide results, but it always took too long. Besides, a stranger just sitting and observing was bound to arouse too much curiosity. And Slocum did not want to hang around too much in Yuma. Someone might come along and recognize him.

In and out fast—that was the ticket.

Besides, a boasting cowhand who had just been paid off and was shooting his mouth off was something so obvious and so common that no one would think twice about it. Perfect camouflage.

The bartender said impassively, "They're gonna 'preciate it, *amigo.*"

"You bet!" Slocum said cheerfully. He drank and let out a rebel yell.

"Your night to howl?" asked the bartender.

"I'm a Texas cowboy an' I eat grizzlies fer breakfast 'n' rattlers fer lunch! Anyone here play poker?"

The bartender sighed. "Friend, at night. People here play poker at night. Too hot jus' now. Why'n't yuh walk 'round the town, take a look at Prison Hill—hell, there ain't nothin' else to look at—an' come back after sundown?"

"Sure," Slocum said agreeably. "How's 'bout leavin' my gear?"

The bartender nodded and reached for the saddlebags. He jerked his head. "Mosey on up Gila Street there," he said. "Don't go an' do nothin' foolish, or you'll wind up inside."

Slocum walked out into the fiery blaze of noon. Adobe houses lined both sides of Gila Street. Dogs panted in the heat in the shadows of the houses, too hot even to bark. The town was waiting for sunset, when it would become alive.

The prison garden was surrounded by massive granite walls thirty feet high. The walls were topped by several strands of vicious barbed wire. The garden was close to the slowly flowing brown river. It had been judged sensible for the prison to grow its own fruit and vegetables rather than haul them in at exorbitant freight rates. The proximity to the river made it easy to irrigate the rows of melons, lettuces, tomatoes, and cucumbers, and to keep the apricot trees in heavy fruit. Everything grew spectacularly with the combination of eternal sunlight and unlimited water.

Slocum walked the perimeter of the bluff. He gawked upwards at the granite walls. His mouth open in wonder, he played the wide-eyed tourist seeing the sights. A guard at one of the guard towers leaned down and yelled, "Keep movin', cowboy!"

Slocum waved and continued his inspection. He had remembered the advice of Joshua Taylor, his old colonel in the cavalry. "John, remember this—time spent in reconnaissance is never wasted. And that's true for business and personal life as well."

He walked to the end of Gila Street, where it stopped at the edge of the Colorado River. Then he turned and walked back again. As he passed under another guard tower, a rifle barrel poked out and kept pace with his sauntering walk. The largest guard tower was high up in the center of the prison. Slocum could see the multiple barrels of a Gatling gun leaning ominously down at the prison yard.

He took the ferry across the river and walked along the eastern shore while he looked over the river side of Prison Hill. There were more guard towers. Slocum took the ferry back to Yuma, thinking hard.

He stared up at the bluff. A man might make it over the wall, but only in a condition of zero visibility, such as in a violent snowstorm. But this was Yuma, where it *never* snowed. A very heavy rainstorm presented possibilities, but it almost never rained.

If Russell Wagner could get to the wall and climb it, Slocum could arrange to be waiting underneath with two horses. But that could only happen if the guards were careless. And it was clear that they were too vigilant for that.

He strolled back to the saloon. The heat was still so strong that a dog lying in the middle of the dusty road refused to get up, even for a heavily loaded wagon. The horses went right over the dog and the broad iron tires crushed the mongrel. No one paid attention. Yuma was not a nice town.

"Been to Prison Hill?" asked the bartender.

Slocum took off his sombrero and wiped his sweating face. He nodded.

"Thirsty work, ain't it?" The bartender drew a beer and set it in front of Slocum.

"Makes a man sorry for the poor bastards in there," he said.

"Hell, I ain't sorry fer 'em," a voice growled at the other end of the dim saloon.

"That's Jim Watts," the bartender said. "He's a guard up there."

"Why ain't you sorry?" asked Slocum.

Watts picked up his glass and slid it along the bar, talking all the while. He turned to Slocum and stared at him with his watery blue eyes. Slocum judged the man to be in his fifties.

"Listen to me, cowboy. We got thirty-four cells. Six bunks to a cell. The hotel is full. Wanna know what the dirty bastards're like? They git to fightin'. We got a special cell for 'em. Fifteen feet square an' ten high. Got rings on the floor. Wanna know what fer? Tell yuh what fer! Them bastards gits to fightin', we chain 'em to the rings so they cain't git at each other. They got to piss, they do it right in their pants. A couple days there, they gits reasonable. Yuma Prison ain't no gals' boardin' school."

Slocum imagined what it must have been like for the spoiled son of a rich man to be dumped into Yuma. If the man had not yet broken under the strain, there was little doubt he was on his way.

He asked casually, "Hey, friend, what about this kid who killed a faro dealer in Tucson? Heard he had a rich daddy."

"Kid's spoiled rotten. Thought he was tough. He don't know what tough is. Got guys in here who kilt people an' then sawed off their fingers to git the rings off. Got a man there who killed his partner up in Kaibab a couple winters ago, nothin' to eat, ate the partner. Got a man who kilt a Navajo sheep-herder fer a two-dollar watch. That Wagner kid's had the shit beaten outa him a couple times. Talked back to me oncet. Laid my club alongside his head. Tol' me his ol' man would run my balls through a wringer. When I finished with 'im he was eddicated somewhat. You betcha!" Watts ended with a satisfied smile.

"How's he now?"

"Quiet. Says nothin'. Looks at the ground a lot. Don't look at no one in the eyes."

Slocum didn't like the sound of that. People as withdrawn as that could go over the edge very easily.

Watts went on. "Besides, the son of a bitch shot a man in the back. He ain't popular. An' he ain't a bad-lookin' feller, an' that makes fer trouble."

Slocum pretended bewilderment. "Trouble?"

"Don't'cha know? Hell, cowboy, where you been all yer life? Men stuck in there fer years, no women? They're gonna turn a nice-lookin' feller like that into a punk. An' what makes it worse is Mrs. Borden." He let out a long whistle. Then he looked up at the clock on the wall. "Time t' get back, cowboy," he said. He slapped half a dollar on the bar and left.

Slocum asked the bartender, "Who's this Mrs. Borden?"

"The superintendent's wife."

"Why that long whistle?"

"You'll know when you see 'er. Hang 'round fer half an hour and you'll git a good view. As soon as it cools off she gits in 'er buggy an' rides 'round Yuma, lettin' us all git a good look."

"What does he mean, she makes it worse?"

The bartender said with disgust, "Hell, man, ain't you ever left nursin' cows? She parades 'round the exercise yard an' the garden an' the mess hall askin' 'em if everythin's all right."

"So what's wrong with that?"

"What's wrong with it? Hell, she don't give a shit 'bout nothin' 'cept drivin' the men crazy with lookin' at her. Her goddamn thievin' husband keeps the food money an' buys diseased cows and wormy beans, that's all he cares about. He ain't takin' care of 'er, yuh know what I mean? So he gives 'er money to go on trips to San Francisco 'n' buy 'er clothes. She hates Yuma. What she does here is show off what she's got."

"And what does she have?" asked Slocum. This couple intrigued him.

"My dad used ter say the prettiest thing in the world was a fat Hereford in a rich pasture. An' the second prettiest was a red-headed woman in a green dress. Miz Borden's got red hair down to 'er hips, if she'd take out them tortoiseshell pins she wears. An' she likes green dresses. Very tight. She don' wear no corsets neither. An' she don't wear *nothin'* underneath them dresses. An' I hear when she walks 'round the garden er 'round the cells she bends down a lot, pretendin' to smell a tomato er see if the cell's been swept, that dress o' hers sorta gits loose 'round 'er boobs. Watts tells me it fair drives 'em crazy. It drives *him* crazy. And he's got a wife at home.

"So now you figger what it does to men who've got years to go inside Prison Hill. I feel kinda sorry fer the kid. There she comes now!"

Slocum turned.

An elegant little buggy drawn by a fine black gelding was moving quickly down Gila Street. The woman holding the reins was wearing a tight green dress. She wore a broad-brimmed hat of yellow straw. A green silk ribbon circled the crown. People turned to watch. The women's faces had a sour expression; the men's were filled with a blend of admiration and lust. Some of the men removed their hats and bowed. To them she inclined her head with a regal gesture.

Even at that distance Slocum could see she wasn't wearing a corset. He could even see the cherry-sized bulges made by her nipples against the tight green fabric. As the buggy moved, the slight bumps of Gila Street made her full breasts jiggle. She carried herself proudly. Her back was straight. She wanted people to see her body.

"Thinks she's a goddamn queen bee," growled the bartender.

"No wonder," Slocum said.

The bartender laughed. Slocum stepped outside the door and stared at the receding buggy. Russell Wagner was having a hard time on Prison Hill. There was no time to plan an elaborate break-out with the well-paid connivance of a guard or two. It would take too much time to find them and then build up the mutual confidence that would be absolutely necessary for that kind of operation.

He turned around and sat down. He cradled his glass in his palms. It was quiet in the saloon now. He could hear the heavy, calm, tick-tock of the grandfather clock next to the big mirror in back of the bar.

It was ticking Russell Wagner's life away.

Every day counted. Slocum sighed. He saw only one possible answer. He had to get into Yuma Territorial Prison, take Russell Wagner with him, and take him out.

And the only way to do that was to commit a felony, plead guilty in order to avoid a time-consuming trial, and get himself sent to Prison Hill.

Slocum got an envelope, paper, and pen from the bartender. He sat down again and wrote:

April 17

Dear Mr. Wagner:

Please be ready to pick up your merchandise exactly three months from the above date.

It will be delivered to the Posada Carapán in Puerto Peñasco, in Old Mexico. It may be necessary for you to wait a few days; some cargoes are difficult to handle. The Posada is very pleasant.

I shall expect full payment on delivery. I shall not accept any excuses for non-payment.

I am, sir,
Very truly yours,
John Slocum

Five minutes later he dropped the letter at the post office. Now he was committed.

2

Juries were usually composed of businessmen. In cattle country, ranchers predominated. Rustling cattle was considered a serious crime. Indeed, murder, if committed in a fair fight, or in self-defense, was considered considerably less worthy of punishment than rustling.

There was no ranching anywhere near Yuma. The Lecheguilla and Yuma Deserts stretched in every direction, and the scarce rainfall would not permit it. So Slocum rented a sorrel gelding named Driscoll. He rode northeast till he arrived at the lush green valleys of the Weaver Mountains. This range stretched to the southwest of Prescott. On the way, since Driscoll had cast a shoe, he stopped in a blacksmith's shop in Wickenburg. When the blacksmith was busy paring Driscoll's hoof, Slocum asked him to make a branding iron.

"What brand?"

"Bar Lazy S."

"Your brand? Never heard of it."

"Just registered it. Startin' my own place other side of Wagoner."

So the blacksmith welded an S on its side to the short horizontal piece for the bar.

That night, over his small cooking fire, Slocum broke off the S between two rocks. Now he had a short bar. This was the working tool of the professional rustler. Its advantage was that this simple horizontal piece of iron could be used to alter just about any brand; the disadvantage was that simple possession of such a tool was *prima facie* evidence of intent to commit a felony—rustling. Any cowpuncher riding his range would shoot any man carrying such a tool, without hesitation.

In the morning Slocum climbed a ridge. He saw a broad valley filled with grazing cattle. They wouldn't do him any good unless there was someone around to see what he was doing and become suspicious.

There was no one in sight. Slocum sighed and moved on to the next ridge. Red dots moved slowly as the cattle grazed. Half hidden behind a small hill which rose in the middle of the valley was a ranch house and a corral. A careless rustler, such as he was pretending to be, approaching the cattle from the north, would not notice the ranch headquarters.

He wet his forefinger and held it up vertically. There was no wind. If a man would make a fire to heat the iron, the smoke would rise straight up in the still air. If he were to make a bigger fire than was necessary, there would be more smoke. And that would attract serious, concerned attention.

A stranger making a fire at suppertime was one thing.

A fire in mid-morning meant a branding fire. It was certain to be investigated immediately.

He picked up an armful of dried piñon branches. He stowed them away in his saddlebag and ran down into the middle of the grazing cattle. They looked at him placidly and continued to munch the grass.

Slocum dismounted and started his fire. He took out the iron and set the bar in the middle of the fire. The smoke rose in a thin grey vertical column. He needed a more dramatic effect. He picked several small bunches of grass with damp soil clinging to their roots and tossed them on the fire.

The resulting black smoke was very gratifying. He lay down a few feet from the fire, clasped his hands behind his neck, and promptly fell asleep. He had ridden hard for three days, and he was exhausted.

Suddenly a jolt of agony shot through his rib cage. Someone had just kicked him viciously with a pointed boot toe.

Three men stood over him. Each rested his right hand on his gun butt. Another man sat his horse to one side. His Winchester rested against the horn, but its muzzle pointed at Slocum's chest.

"You ain't movin', son," the horseman said coldly.

"Nope," Slocum said.

"Git up."

Slocum sat up. The fire had burned out. Resting in the still-warm ashes was the iron. The four men were looking at it.

"Git his gun."

One man reached down and jerked out Slocum's Colt. Then they stepped back. They were giving the horseman a clear field of fire. The horseman, a man of sixty with white hair, said quietly, "Ride aroun' an' see did he change any brand. You, you son of a bitch, keep sittin' or I'll blow yuh into doll rags.''

"Yes, sir," Slocum said, with a deliberately respectful tone.

"I got half a mind to blow your fuckin' head off, you goddamn cow thief. But first I wanna know how many you altered. What's your name?"

"Dick Prendergast."

"Where you hail from, Dick?"

"Snake River country."

"Who were you gonna sell 'em to?"

"Hell, no one."

"Startin' your own little spread, hey?"

Slocum shrugged.

"You a Johnny Reb?"

"West Virginia."

"I thought I heard somethin' southrun. I fought you grey-backs fer four years." His voice seemed to get friendlier. "So yuh fell asleep, hey?" the man went on. "You asshole." But his anger had lessened. "Yo're the wust goddamn rustler I ever did see." He shook his head and relaxed his grip on the carbine. "An' start a fuckin' forest fire c'n be seen two hunnert miles! An' my ranch house is just over the hill yonder!" He shook his head in amazement.

"Your ranch house is where?" asked Slocum, with an annoyed tone.

"Jus' beyont that hill."

"Ah, shit," Slocum said, with a note of rueful anger.

The men rode back. One said, "Nope. He didn't touch none of 'em. What he did, he rode down from the end of the ridge there, started a brandin' fire right in the middle of that bunch. Din't even git to rope a single one. Started the fire, stuck his iron in, an' *fell asleep.*"

Everyone started to laugh. Even Slocum joined in, with the proper sheepish expression. The rancher stopped laughing abruptly.

"Git on your hoss."

Slocum mounted. One of the men took a piggin string from his back pocket and proceeded to lash his wrists to the saddle horn.

"You're lucky the old man didn't kill yuh right off," he said.

Slocum shrugged. That was a chance he had to take. He had been very careful not to change a single brand, on the principle that a contemplated felony was not as seriously regarded as a completed one.

At Wickenburg the indictment was followed by his guilty plea, much to the astonishment of his court-appointed lawyer, who told Slocum that if he pleaded not guilty, he had an excellent chance of winning and going free.

The judge immediately sentenced him to four years at Yuma Territorial Prison. All of these procedures took place within two weeks. The judge was amazed to see a smile spread across the prisoner's face when he pronounced the words "Yuma Territorial Prison." He called Slocum's lawyer up and quietly asked him if his client were insane. "I don't think so," the lawyer said unhappily. "He's just unusual."

"But is he unusual enough so that I can have him committed to the insane asylum? I find his reaction to the sentence rather striking."

"Let me talk to him, Your Honor."

Slocum simply said, "Go away."

So, one hour later, Slocum was handcuffed and placed between two deputies, who escorted him to Yuma in the stagecoach. The road went alongside the Hassayampa, then joined the old road north of the Gila.

Almost three weeks from the time when he first walked by Prison Hill, Slocum entered through the gates. They clanged shut behind him.

As one deputy watched the superintendent sign the receipt for the prisoner he whispered to Slocum, "This super is a son of a bitch. Watch your step. Don' talk back, an' do your time easy. Four years ain't so bad. Don' let that son of a bitch ketch you lookin' at his wife, or you'll wind up in the snake pit. Good luck. If you're gonna rustle some more, don't fall asleep, an' go do it out of the territory. The judge is hell on repeaters."

Slocum nodded. He was looking up at a window in the superintendent's quarters. A hand had pushed the lace curtains back. A woman in a green dress was looking down at him.

"That's who I mean," whispered the deputy. "Judith Borden is the biggest bitch in Arizona Territory. *Watch your step.*"

Superintendent Borden looked up from the documents that had travelled with the deputy sheriffs. He leaned back in his oak chair and placed his big white hands flat on the cluttered oak desk in front of him. A dead fern slumped in a discouraged manner on the dusty windowsill.

"We got some rules here," he said. He had big, beefy shoulders. Slocum thought that if the man had been wearing a white apron he would look like a butcher. Slocum smiled at the thought.

"One rule is, don't give me shit-faced grins, like what you're doin' right now. Wipe it off."

"Sure," Slocum said. He wiped the grin off.

"Take your hands out of your pockets when I or any guard talks to you. And every time you say something to me or any guard, I want to hear a 'sir' tacked on. Got that?"

Slocum nodded.

The superintendent waited.

"Sir," Slocum added.

Two guards stood in back of Slocum. Both carried oak clubs two feet long.

"Don't slump!" said the superintendent. His face began to redden. "Stand at attention!"

"Like this, sir?" Slocum asked. He stood at attention.

Borden nodded. He bent his head to examine Slocum's documents.

The bigger guard, a man named Perkins, leaned over and hissed into Slocum's left ear, "You're a right smart feller, ain't'cha? Don't come over me with that, er you'll be sorry you was ever born."

Slocum paid no attention. He felt a painful jab to his left kidney. Perkins had driven the end of his club into Slocum's back with a sudden, vicious blow.

"Unnerstan'?" Perkins whispered.

Slocum turned slowly and stared at him. There was something so cold and hard in Slocum's green-eyed gaze that Perkins felt his self-confidence waver. But Perkins had seen hard men come into Yuma, and he had reduced them to grovelling. It was not too hard if a man knew what to do.

"Take yer hands outa yer pockets, you son of a bitch," Borden grated. His face paled and he jerked his head at the two guards.

Slocum promptly removed his hands. This was no time to show independence.

The color came back to the superintendent's face. The guards sighed and relaxed. Slocum noticed that they seemed disappointed at not being able to use their oak clubs. Perkins kept slapping his club against his palm.

"You stand at attention whenever I or a guard talks to you! Got that straight?"

"Sure," Slocum said agreeably.

"It's yessir!" Perkins hissed in his ear. He jabbed his club once more into Slocum's side. Once more Slocum turned and looked at the man.

"Keep lookin' at Mr. Borden!" Perkins said. "An' Perkins is my name. You're gonna hear it plenty 'roun' here."

Borden said, "You just touch—I mean *touch*—a guard, and you'll do one month in solitary on bread and water. No light. You got that?"

"An' rats too," Perkins said. "Rats big as cats."

Slocum nodded. "Big as cats," he said. "Gotcha."

Perkins grabbed his hair from behind and said, "It's 'yessir' an' 'nosir'. So what's it gonna be? Don' start off on the wrong foot, er you'll regret it."

Borden watched with approval. Slocum decided that Perkins would be the one to do some regretting. But that would come in good time. This kind of bullying could not occur without the approval of the superintendent, who was watching with his eyes bright. It was clear that the guards took their cues from Borden. Perkins jerked his head back with a vicious snap.

"I see that we're goin' to have trouble from you," Borden said.

"No, sir," Slocum said. It would be stupid to start off his stay in Yuma with solitary confinement when the only essential thing was to get Russell Wagner and plan a quick break-out.

"That's better," Borden said. He nodded toward the guards.

"Let's go," Perkins snapped. He had heavy-lidded eyes, thick lips that curved downward, and eyes of a washed-out blue. The other guard was Frank Reed. Reed was a short, fat man with heavily muscled forearms. The arms were tattooed with crossed anchors and buxom mermaids. He had once sailed on the Bering Sea whalers, before he ended up at Yuma. He hated the town and the prisoners he guarded.

Once outside the room, Perkins shoved Slocum roughly. "Move, *move!*" he shouted.

Slocum controlled himself. Perkins kept shoving him down the length of the hall, around a corner, and halfway down a corridor. Finally Perkins gave a heavy thrust that sent Slocum almost stumbling into a small room with a wide wooden counter stretching across the end closest to the door. Slocum caught himself against the counter with an audible thump. He did not turn around to look at Perkins. He was afraid that if he caught sight of that hated face he might lose control of himself and ruin everything. So he stood with his arms braced against the counter.

In back of the counter, an old man slowly stood up. He had been reading a newspaper. This he carefully folded and placed on one of the wooden shelves that ran down the length of the room. He had been sitting on a tall stool. His closely cropped white hair grew on top of a narrow, withered face. He was wearing a jacket of a coarse cotton fabric which Slocum deduced was the top half of the prison uniform.

"Here's one fer yuh, Bob," Perkins said. The old man grunted.

He sized up Slocum, nodded, and turned to get him his outfit. As soon as his back was turned Slocum saw the white circle, six inches across, that had been sewn on to the center of the back of the jacket. It would make a perfect target for a man with a rifle, even in the dusk. Perkins grinned at Reed and nodded. Reed lifted his oak club and brought it down on the counter as hard as he could.

The old man leaped with fright. The two guards dissolved into laughter and turned to leave.

"Always getcha, Bob," Perkins said.

"That you do," the old man said. He smiled, but Slocum could see the hatred that boiled in the old man's eyes.

He turned to Slocum. "I'm the storekeeper. I'm Bob Tolliver. Strip, son."

"Strip?"

"Bare-ass naked, boy. Like a blue jay without feathers. Put everythin' on the counter."

Slocum stripped. Tolliver said, "You're pretty well chewed up there, ain't'cha?"

Slocum nodded. Tolliver tossed a jute sack on the counter. Slocum put everything inside the sack. "Funny feller, that Perkins," he said.

"Rotten, yeller-belly bastard! Effen I was younger I woulda jumped 'im, nemmin' the snake pit."

"What's this snake pit?"

"Oh, that's *bad*, that place. Big cell blasted outa granite. They shackle your hands an' feet to ring bolts in the floor. Bread an' water. When you gotta piss, you piss in your pants."

Tolliver wrote on a tag. He tied it to the sack and then stowed it away on a shelf in the back of the storeroom. "You'll get it back when you leave."

Then he looked at Slocum. "Smile, God damn it, mister, you're in for four. Smile!"

Slocum did not smile. Tolliver added, "I'm in fer life." Without a change of expression he said, eyeing Slocum critically, "Feet size eleven?" Slocum nodded. Tolliver pulled out a pair of rough cowhide shoes. He tossed them to Slocum. He went to another shelf and pulled out a pair of grey cotton pants and a grey cotton jacket.

The shoes were spattered with dark brown spots. While Slocum dressed, Tolliver said, "That's blood. Feller who owned 'em tried to climb the wall last month."

"They put him in the snake pit an' beat 'im?" Slocum asked.

"Christ, no. The Gatling gun on the guard tower blew 'im to rags. He's in the cemetery next to the river. Got hisself a redwood slab with his name on it. You thinkin' 'bout goin' over the wall?"

Slocum shrugged and tied his shoelaces.

"Ev'ryone thinks 'bout it at first. Them as tries it winds up with them redwood slabs, er the Yumas drag 'em in."

"Yumas?"

"Christ, where you been? The Yumas—the Injuns 'round here. They know the desert real good. They git fifty bucks when they bring in a prisoner. Men c'n buy a lot of firewater with fifty bucks. Buy hisself a pretty squaw, too. So what happens? A man takes to readin' the Holy Book, or says, 'Shit, I'll go over the wall.' Or some of 'em starts to laugh an' cry. It makes the other men mighty nervous. So then he gits put in solitary, where his screamin' won't bother nobody."

"They put a crazy man in solitary?"

"If they don't, someone's gonna git a knife an' kill 'im fer some quiet. So the superintendent slaps 'em in solitary. An' then a lot of 'em just cracks they heads open 'gainst the rock."

Slocum let out a long breath.

Tolliver said, "Come back in four years 'n' git your gear. An' now come with me. I'm takin' you to the jute shop."

Rows of men sat at long tables. As Slocum entered they raised their heads to stare at the new man. Two small barred windows high up in the thick stone wall let in shafts of yellow sunlight. The big room was thick with the acrid stench of sweat-soaked clothes. Two guards stood at each end of the room, facing each other.

One guard stepped forward as soon as he noticed Slocum. It was Perkins.

"All right," he said to Tolliver, and jerked his thumb at the door. Tolliver went. Perkins turned toward Slocum and snapped, "You! Take off your cap."

Slocum looked at him.

"Now!"

Slocum took off the cap. Perkins looked at the tall man with the hard-bitten, closed face. He knew there would be trouble here unless he moved first to show who was boss.

"Whenever you see me, you take off yer cap. Got that?"

"Yep."

"'Yes, sir'!"

"Sure, yessir."

Perkins was mollified. "An' when you pass by, then you put it on again. Got that?"

"Yes, sir."

"Good." Perkins smiled. He had dominated the son of a bitch right away, and there shouldn't be any trouble later on. And, if there was trouble, he could handle it. The man looked subdued.

"Sit down at that chair. You, make room! Ever handle a needle?"

"No, sir."

"Good. I'll make a seamstress outa you, cowboy. I think we'll git along. Wagner!"

Slocum's eyes widened. He looked up and down the long, silent rows where the prisoners sat stitching jute bags together from piles of the coarse jute fabric. He was curious whether he could pick out Russell Wagner by himself, before the man responded. The faces he scanned were scornful, or impassive, or resigned. The fingers kept busy with their sewing with the long, thick needles.

Slocum's swift gaze stopped at a man with a haggard, thin face who was bent over his sewing. His eyes were not focused on his work, but seemed to be looking at something a vast distance away. Slocum guessed that was Wagner.

"*Wagner!*"

Wagner's head lifted. It seemed to Slocum that it took a lot of effort. Finally the eyes focused on Perkins. Then Wagner stood up. His head hung down as he stared at the ground.

"Yes, sir," he mumbled.

Perkins turned toward Slocum. "You take a lesson from Wagner, now," he said with a complacent smirk. "He come in here actin' all-fired important. It took only a couple weeks before he got polite. Ain't that right?"

A scab was healing high up on Russell Wagner's left cheek. It would be the kind of mark left by a club, Slocum decided. His right cheek under his eye was swollen just about where a left-handed man would have struck him with a fist. Perkins was left-handed.

"I ast a question, Russell, boy," Perkins said in a menacing tone.

Heads suddenly turned to watch. The distant look faded out of Wagner's eyes. With a visible effort he looked at Perkins. He spoke in a low, sullen monotone.

"Yes, sir."

The stench of sweat in the room, which was a hundred and twenty degrees by now, was overpowering. No one seemed to notice.

Slocum let out an inward sigh of relief. He had been afraid for a moment that Wagner might have become so

brutalized in his brief stay that he had become apathetic.
The tone of his voice told Slocum that there was still anger
there, although it was being suppressed.

Perkins turned back to Slocum. "All right, cowboy. Sit
next to Mr. Wagner there. That'll be yer seat from now on.
Don' let me ketch you sittin' in another seat. They'll tell
yuh I like things neat an' reg'lar. Sit!"

Slocum compressed his lips. No one had ever ordered
him around as if he were a trained dog. He kept his face
impassive and clamped a firm control on the rage that was
welling up. But, as Wagner slid over to make room for him,
he smiled. He was in luck, after all. On his first day on
Prison Hill, he had been given a place beside Russell Wagner.

"What yuh smilin' fer? Wipe it off!"

"Yes, sir," Slocum said promptly.

Perkins grunted and left the room.

Wagner said contemptuously, without looking up, "You
learn fast. You only been here five minutes and you're
already kissin' ass."

"That's the way to get on in this world," Slocum said
equably.

"It ain't my way!"

"Learn it, son."

Someone tittered.

Wagner flushed. "Don't call me 'son,' you son of a bitch!"

The room fell silent. Heads turned to see what the new
man would do.

Slocum knew he would have a hard time of it unless he
responded quickly and effectively. Without a second's hesitation he slapped Russell's right cheek as hard as he could.
Russell recovered and swung an overhand right which Slocum allowed to strike on the left side of his jaw. Slocum

toppled over backward and hit the floor. The prisoners' shouts of encouragement brought Perkins in at the run.

He bent down and grabbed Slocum by the back of his jacket. "Startin' up already?" he screamed. He shook Slocum as if the new man were a puppy that had just messed up a new rug. Slocum had never let anyone do such a thing to him. He relaxed and let himself be shaken.

"Let me at that bastard!" he yelled.

The other guard had Russell in an unnecessary headlock.

"I'll show you two pricks to start trouble!" Perkins yelled with a red, sweating face. "Stick 'em in together!"

Slocum concealed his pleasure. Perkins would have changed his decision immediately if he had the least suspicion that Slocum welcomed this chance to talk with Wagner in complete privacy.

3

"Three days on bread 'n' water, you assholes," Perkins growled as he slammed the heavy cell door. With a wide grin of satisfaction, he locked the door with one of the keys that hung from a ring at his belt.

Slocum listened to the steps of the guards moving away. It was four in the afternoon and the stone walls and floor had absorbed the heat of the desert day. All night long the stone would radiate out the heat it had stored. There would be no coolness at all. They would sweat without ceasing. And all they had to drink each twenty-four hours was one pint of water.

He looked up. Light poured in through a barred window twenty feet up on one wall. The window was too small for anyone to scrape through. He and Russell were manacled by their wrists and ankles to massive ring bolts set deep in the stone floor.

Slocum said quietly, "Anyone able to hear what I say when I talk like this?"

"Yell your fuckin' head off. Nobody'll come till they bring us a hunk of bread and some water tomorrow mornin'."

His voice was sullen, which seemed to be its constant tone. Slocum felt the back of his jacket and trousers beginning to turn soggy with sweat.

"You know why I'm here?" Slocum asked quietly. His crisp, efficient tone startled Wagner. Up to now Slocum had played the role of an amiable, cowardly bungler whose inept rustling technique would soon be spread throughout Prison Hill. The fact that he had suddenly flared up at an insult from another prisoner would not be out of character.

"Sure. You swung at me an' I swung back."

"No, Russell. I'm here to get you out of Yuma."

Russell's mouth opened. He shut it again and turned his head to stare at Slocum.

Then he said with finality, "You're crazy as a bedbug. Don't talk to me no more," and turned his head away.

But there was something about the absolute still calm of the tall man chained beside him which did not jibe with any kind of insane behavior he had ever seen—and he had seen quite a lot of it in his short time in the prison. He turned toward Slocum once more and waited.

"Shall I go on?" Slocum asked.

Russell shrugged.

"Your father is paying me to get you out of here."

"Oh, shit," Russell said in disbelief.

Slocum waited patiently. Russell couldn't think of anything to say. He stared at the granite roof. He turned his head sideways and looked at Slocum. Then he thought, *Maybe it's true*.

"Listen," he began, "what's your name?"

"John's good enough."

"Listen, John, you're loco. Or my father is."

"Or both of us," Slocum said calmly.

"Or that prick Borden sent you here to try somethin'."

"What?"

"I can't think why, but he's a mean bastard."

"I'll go along with that. And when you figure out what he's trying to do by sending me in here, why, you just let me know. In the meantime I'm gonna grab me some shut-eye."

Five minutes passed. Wagner thought hard. Finally he said, "Hey, John, wake up. I can't figger it out. But there's no way to get outa here. No one escapes from Yuma. You're even wearin' the shoes of a guy who tried it last. Used to be the gardener here. Nice job, too. Got to eat fresh tomatoes and stuff. Had two more years to go, but even he couldn't take it no more. Smart guy, too. He got chewed up by that Gatlin' gun they got in the tower. You can't go over the wall. You can't go through it."

Slocum noticed that he hadn't said, "You can't go under." That was something to keep in mind.

Aloud he said, "Maybe. Think you can handle the next four years?"

"Christ, no! I been beat up twice. Some guys tried to make me a punk. Next time they try I'm gonna kill one of 'em."

"Then they'll hang you."

"I don't give a shit!"

And suddenly tears trickled from the corners of Wagner's eyes. Slocum pretended not to notice. Things were really getting serious with Russell Wagner. There had to be action, and fast.

"I'll find a way out," Slocum said calmly. He hoped that his quiet assurance would encourage Wagner to hold on.

"You're a lyin' bastard. Don't talk to me!"

Slocum waited.

Wagner stared at the ceiling. "What's my father look like?" he suddenly demanded.

Slocum said, "About five nine. Weight, about two hundred. Little pot belly. Grey eyes. Hair grey as well. Narrow forehead. Smokes expensive cigars. Wears a grey Stetson. He—"

"That's enough. You coulda seen 'im somewhere."

"True. Then he told me you're allowed to get one letter a month."

"Yeah. So what?"

Everything Wagner said held a note of challenge.

"You get the letters on the last day of each month."

"Yeah." Again Wagner's voice was full of contemptuous arrogance. He had recovered from his temporary weakness.

"That's tomorrow."

Wagner grunted. "Guys in the snake den don't get nothin' 'cept bread 'n' water. So I don't get mail till I get out."

Slocum's eyes were closed. "In three days you'll be reading a letter from your dad. It will say, 'You will be talking to a friend of mine. Trust him.'"

Wagner was silent. How could this stranger know what his father had written unless he had spoken to him? Any other explanation would be too crazy.

"An' you're this friend, hey?"

Slocum nodded.

"I like to pick my own friends."

Slocum said, "Are you this stupid all the time?"

Wagner blew up. He began to scream hoarsely in an uncontrollable rage. He said how much he'd like to get his hands on Slocum and how much pleasure it would give him to do it.

Slocum waited patiently with his eyes closed. When Wagner finally ran out of steam Slocum said, with an icy calm so chilling that even Wagner felt it would be best to obey: *"Shut up."*

For the next three days Slocum did not say a word. Somehow Wagner was impressed by this grim silence in a way he could not explain. He tried, late on the second day, to be friendly. Each time he made an approach the tall man with the hard green eyes looked at him briefly and with mild interest, as if Wagner were a strange insect mounted with a pin under a glass cover.

Each time, Wagner flushed. He responded to this humiliation by determining to be as unpleasant as possible.

On the fourth morning, Perkins and Reed came in. They unlocked the wrist and ankle manacles.

When Wagner started to enter his cell, Perkins gave him a hard shove along the corridor.

"Ain't I goin' in?"

"They're searchin' all the cells," Reed said abruptly. "In case you guys got a cute surprise hidden there somewheres. Out in the yard. On the double!"

As Wagner turned, Reed said, "Here. Got a letter for yuh."

Superintendent Borden had already read the letter; afterwards, deciding that it was harmless, he had folded over the open end and sent it down.

Slocum watched Wagner squat in the tiny exercise yard. His fingers trembled slightly. He extracted the note and read it. Then he put the note back, refolded the flap, and stuck the letter in his hip pocket.

"Well?" Slocum asked, standing above him with his hands in his pockets.

Wagner said flatly, "All right."

"Satisfied?"

"Yeah."

Slocum walked back and forth with his hands in his pockets. Coming back and standing over Wagner, who was drawing aimless circles in the dust with a forefinger, he said, "We're going to move as soon as I get an idea that's goin' to work. If we start there'll be no turning back. Agreed?"

"Yeah. But I got to agree first. Right?"

Slocum stared down at Wagner's bent head. This last remark meant that Wagner felt he had to exercise control. This had to be cleared up right away.

"Russell," Slocum said softly. Three prisoners were tossing a ball back and forth. They jeered loudly whenever one of them dropped it. The muzzle of the Gatling high up in the main guard tower was pointing down at them.

"Russell. Let's get one thing straight right now. We don't move out till you agree it looks good. We're together on that. Sure we are. But once we're agreed, you do as I say and no arguments."

"What are you, a general or something? That's my old man's money payin' for this, I bet!"

His voice had risen. Two nearby prisoners turned to look.

"Quietly, you damn fool," Slocum said with a friendly smile. Russell simmered down, aware he had been foolishly talking too loudly. "As for your thinkin' I'm a general, why, yes, I reckon I am. Yes, I'm the general of an army with only one private. I guess you could say that. But if you want out, that's the way it has to be. Yes or no?"

Russell tossed a small pebble in the air a few times, thinking hard.

"My old man ain't a fool," he said finally. "He don't piss his money away. He knows what he's doin'. So I guess I gotta trust you."

"Good."

"But I don't like it."

"Who said you had to like it?" Slocum said placidly.

Mrs. Borden watched Slocum the way she looked at all newly arrived prisoners. When he smiled she noticed that his face lighted up. She found the harsh outlines of his tanned face suddenly very attractive. She watched carefully and found herself staring at his crotch. The bulge excited her. She could do a lot of favors for him, and, if he had any sense, he would know what she would expect of him in return.

The garden! Yes, it would have to be the garden. She had needed a new gardener ever since the old one had been killed going over the wall. The tomatoes were now choked with weeds, which grew profusely in the blend of heat and plentiful water pumped up from the river to run in narrow irrigation ditches. The weeds were now as tall as the tomato plants; the slugs were eating up the lettuces.

The best thing about the garden—as far as she was concerned—was the shack built at one corner. The shack had been built against the high granite rock face on which the prison proper had been built. The stone wall continued around the garden, and the central guard tower could see anyone working in the garden, but—and this was a big but—no one could see the shack from the prison or from the tower.

Moreover, a flight of steps led down to the garden, and anyone walking down the steps could be noticed immediately. There could be no one sneaking up on the shack if the people inside were reasonably vigilant.

Right next to the shack there was a hand pump. Whoever

was gardener had to pump the water up from the river from a narrow pipe which went over the wall and down thirty feet to the river, where it was submerged deep enough to suck up the water, no matter what level the Colorado happened to be. The guard tower knew that a man could shinny up the wall by clinging to the pipe, so it was kept under constant observation whenever anyone was in the garden.

The shack was well equipped with rakes, hoes, spades and shovels, burlap bags, and tomato stakes. The sacks were above young seedlings to shield them from the ferocious sun. Plenty of sacks, she thought. Enough to make an impromptu bed.

There was also an old tin washtub, which one of the previous gardeners had had a guard bring in from outside. It had become the right of each gardener, in turn, to use it as his own washtub when he wanted to sluice off the dust and sweat. It was very nice to have a clean, freshly soaped man to poise himself above her when she lay on her back on the sacks.

It was her duty to make tours of inspection of the garden from time to time to see how the current gardener was doing. At that time she would pick the fruits and vegetables that would be served that day at her table. The remainder of the harvest was never sent to the prison kitchen; it was sold in town for the superintendent's benefit.

When she fantasized what she and the new prisoner could be doing on a pile of sacks in the gardener's shack, she squeezed her thighs together. Suddenly she was wet.

"Darling," she said.

"What?" Borden asked. He had been bent over a plate. It was filled with a steak, freshly sliced tomatoes, and freshly boiled corn slathered with butter. He ate like a pig. She suppressed a vicious comment.

"We need a new gardener. The garden's full of weeds and the irrigation ditches have to be opened up."

"Tell Perkins to put someone there."

"All right."

She went out and walked to the guards' room. Perkins got lazily to his feet and wiped his mouth. He had been eating.

"Yes'm?"

"Mr. Borden wants that new man to be tried out as a gardener."

"But—" Perkins had his eye on someone else who had promised that he would give the guard the best tomatoes and watermelons if Perkins got him the job.

"No buts. The new prisoner. See to it."

When she left Perkins muttered *"Bitch!"* under his breath. This was the first time that the Superintendent had ever usurped Perkins's prerogative. Perkins didn't like it.

The men looked up from stitching away at the bags.

"You!" Perkins said, with an angry tone. He pointed at Slocum.

Slocum stood up and said, "Yes, sir."

"You're the new gardener. Go out there an' git to work."

At that time Slocum did not know that Mrs. Borden had, unwittingly, just handed him and Wagner their tickets to escape.

4

Slocum enjoyed pulling weeds. He liked to hoe between the rows of corn and tomatoes. He liked the pungent smell of the tomato plants. He delighted in the daily bath in the washtub.

On the second day, Borden emerged from his office and watched Slocum work for a few minutes. "Good work," he grunted.

Slocum removed his hat and said, "Thank you, sir."

"Thought in the beginnin' you was gonna be a hardcase," Borden said. "But you buckled down real good." He looked at the pile of weeds. "I'll tell Perkins to get someone to get rid of 'em."

"No, sir. I can use 'em."

"Use *weeds?* How?"

"Chop 'em up and set 'em between the rows for a mulch."

"A what?"

It was clear to Slocum that Borden knew nothing about gardening. This was information that could be useful later on.

"Mulch, sir. Keeps the ground damp and keeps other weeds from takin' hold. Also, it rots an' makes good fertilizer."

Borden smiled thinly. "You're doin' good work. Keep it up! Feller before you wasn't good at it. We're gonna have a good tomato crop, looks like."

Tomatoes brought in a lot of money in the Yuma market, Slocum knew. And it all went into Borden's pocket. Here was Slocum's chance to work on his escape plan, which had suddenly sprung into his mind while he was spading up a ruined irrigation ditch.

"Yes, sir. Cucumbers comin' along fine, too. I could almost double the crop if I had some help."

"Fine. I'll tell Perkins to send someone." Borden turned to go.

"Sir, if I can make a suggestion..."

Borden turned. "Yeah?" He was pleased with Slocum's work.

"Best if I work with someone I get along with."

"Sure, sure. Who you got in mind?"

"Russell Wagner."

"That snotty shit? You had a fight with 'im an' wound up in the snake den!"

"Yes, sir. But we became friends down there. He'll work hard."

"Don't look like it to me. Always mopin' an' bitchin'."

Slocum said grimly, "He'll work hard. I'll see to that."

Borden looked again at the neat rows Slocum had been working on. He looked at the freshly staked tomato plants. Earlier, they had sprawled every which way. All of them were now upright. Slocum had already filled two bushels with ripe tomatoes without being asked to do so.

Borden liked a man who knew how to take initiative.

"All right," he finally said. "I'll see to it." He turned and walked away. Slocum began weeding the rows behind the shack. From his office Borden looked down at him with approval. Judith Borden came and stood beside him.

"Good worker," Borden said.

Judith Borden stared at Slocum's broad back. It was glistening with sweat and his big shoulder muscles jumped as he pulled weeds. She felt the preliminary excitement that meant she wanted a man. Her nipples swelled at the mere thought of those broad shoulders bearing down on her. Where? In the shack? Somehow she would have to work it out.

"I like good workers," she said.

Neither of them knew what Slocum was really doing as he went on pulling up the weeds. He was carefully measuring the distance from the back of the shack to the wall.

Wagner examined his hands. Large blisters were ballooning up on the palms.

"Jesus!" he complained. He threw down his hoe.

"Pick it up," Slocum said quietly.

"Why? You doin' me a favor, gettin' me a job in this goddamn garden workin' like a peon?"

"You'd rather be sewin' jute bags?"

"You're goddamn right! It ain't hot like this an' i c'n sit down without the sun burnin' me up." He crossed his arms and glowered at Slocum. "Fuck this." He turned to go.

"Russell," Slocum said softly.

Wagner stopped reluctantly. He sensed the steel behind the soft voice. Slocum had been planning to talk to Wagner during the noon break, but it had better be now.

"If we work hard here, Borden will be pleased. And we'll be in good physical condition."

"Condition for what?" Wagner asked with sarcasm. "Gettin' a job in a truck farm when we get out?"

"No, Russell," Slocum said softly, "for crossing the desert when we escape. I have it all planned."

"Jesus! How?" Wagner asked, staring at Slocum.

"It's fifteen feet from the back of the shack to the wall. You better pick up the hoe an' work while we're talkin'. Borden can see us any time he looks out his window."

"You ain't goin' over the wall! No one ever went over the wall!"

"We're not goin' over the wall," Slocum said patiently. "An' don't keep choppin' at the same place with that hoe. Keep movin' along, like I am."

"That guard up in the tower c'n see ev'ry bit of this garden! An' we ain't ever gonna be here at night, neither."

"Yes," Slocum said with the same patient tone. "Now, Brother Wagner, if I can continue."

"Yeah, go ahead." Wagner leaned on his hoe.

"First, since someone's probably watchin' us right now, let's get to work."

Wagner reluctantly picked up his hoe.

"And we're goin' to work hard. *Real hard.*"

"Not me."

"Oh, yes, you are, Brother Wagner. An' I'll tell you why."

"Yeah?" Wagner spoke with a challenging tone. "Why?"

"Because if we work real hard in the sun they're not gonna object if we rest in the shack from eleven to two."

No one ever did physical labor in the open air during the hottest hours of the day.

"Right?" Slocum asked.

Wagner nodded grudgingly.

"An' durin' those three hours of siesta," Slocum went on, "you an' me will dig a tunnel."

"A *what?*"

"Keep your voice down, Brother Wagner. A tunnel. We dig down six feet. Then we pitch 'er downward at a thirty-degree angle. That will take us under the wall footing. We keep goin' a few feet more, and we'll come out a couple feet under the top of the Colorado River."

Wagner stared at him.

"Keep hoein'! We'll float down the river till we're past the town. Then we strike across the Yuma Desert till we hit Mexico."

Staring at the ground as he hoed inexpertly, Wagner said, "I can't swim fer shit."

"I'll figure somethin' out."

Wagner said, as if the thought had just struck him, "Mexico? Across the *desert?*"

"Yep."

This dry stretch of southwest Arizona had one road. It came from Chihuahua and angled to the northwest on its way to California. The early Spanish explorers had quickly christened it *El Camino del Diablo*—the Devil's Road. Thousands had died of thirst and Apache raids as they struggled across the waterless sandy and stony wastes.

Wagner's face looked pinched and a bit frightened. He tried hard not to show it. "That's real bad country."

"Right," Slocum said cheerfully. "That's why they'll expect us to go another way."

"But—"

"There's lots of buts, Russell. We'll handle 'em as they come along. But well have to be in good condition to make it, you see?"

"Sure," Wagner said slowly. "Sure."

Borden watched the two men as they hoed with vigor. It made him hot just to look at them. He waved his fan and took a drink of cool water from the clay *olla* that hung suspended in a corner of his office. A damp burlap wrapped around it kept the *olla's* contents cool by evaporation. When eleven o'clock came they dropped their hoes and entered the shack. *Hell*, Borden thought, *let 'em take it easy for a while*. They were sweating profusely.

If they kept it up, the way they're going, he thought with satisfaction, *I'll have bumper crops and that'll mean a few hundred dollars more in my pocket*.

Inside the shack Slocum said, "Sit down so you c'n see if anyone's comin'. Hold this shovel in your lap an' file away at it."

"What the hell fer?"

Slocum sighed. He wanted to say sharply, "Because I say so, you shithead!" Instead he said patiently, "When you see someone comin' you just stop filin'. That'll give me enough time to straighten out the tunnel. All right?"

Wagner nodded and took the file.

Slocum pushed the empty sacks aside from the wall. He shoved the washtub to one side of the place he had chosen as the entrance point of his vertical shaft. The washtub was wide enough to cover the opening.

"Hey, Mr. Slocum," Wagner said scornfully, "you forgot somethin'."

"What?"

"How we gonna get rid of all that dirt? Pile it in a corner till we crawl out?"

"Pardner," Slocum said gently as he picked up a shovel and began digging, "what we take out is dirt. And what is a garden?"

"Huh?"

"It's dirt. So we spread it 'round the garden, little by little."

"But it's gonna be a diff'rent color," Wagner said, almost triumphantly. "Them guards might be stupid, but they ain't that stupid!"

Slocum looked at him for a moment.

"So," Wagner finished, waving his file, "it'll show up in a second."

"Nope," Slocum said, tossing out a shovelful of the hard-packed clay soil. "Nope."

"An' why the hell not?" Wagner demanded. Slocum's assurance angered him.

"Because, friend Wagner, we'll be busy spadin' the new dirt right back into the old. We'll really mix it in. An' you want to bet that Borden will love it? He'll see us workin' hard, improvin' the soil an' all. He'll *love* it. Hand me that pick-ax."

"Clay? We're gonna be workin' in *clay?*"

"Yep," Slocum said cheerfully.

"But that's gonna be hard to work! What're you so happy about?"

"Because, *amigo mio*, that means we don't have to figger out how to get any lumber to shore up the tunnel. Which we'd have to do if we had sand all the way. With clay we just dig an' it won't collapse on us. Keep your eye on the steps out there, damn it."

Wagner stared at him sullenly.

"Keep watch, damn you!" Slocum said, with a harsh intensity. Wagner decided he had better do so.

The inside of the shack was hot and airless. In two hours, using the pick-ax to break up the clay and the shovel to throw out the excavated soil, the two men had dug down four feet. That was all Slocum needed for the vertical shaft. From then on the tunnel would pitch down at a thirty-degree angle. It was time for a dry run on his alarm system.

"Just tap that file on the shovel when I'm in the shaft," Slocum said.

He found he could scramble out, pull the washtub over the shaft entrance, and toss the empty sacks on the excavated dirt in fifteen seconds. It took a man walking to the shack from the prison door just twenty seconds to arrive at the door of the shack. Slocum had timed that distance earlier.

What would happen when either he or Wagner was deep inside the tunnel? That was a problem that would have to be solved when the time came. Luckily, Wagner was not thinking that far ahead, or else he would have made some sort of sneering remark about that, and Slocum had had enough of that kind of talk for the day.

As for getting the dirt distributed in the garden, that was easy enough. Each man would tie the bottom of his pants legs, pour dirt inside, and as he walked along the rows of plants, he would loose the knot and let the dirt dribble slowly past his ankles. Then he would spade it into the old dirt. Slocum laid out this plan in detail.

"What about light in the tunnel?" Wagner asked.

"Candles."

"Yeah. Well, all right," Wagner said in a grudging tone. He never said anything showing approval, but he was always fast to point out defects. Slocum told himself that he must keep his temper with the kid. It would be hard, but there would be a lot of money if this all worked out.

Control, control. And careful planning.

On the way back to their cells Perkins told them sourly, "I gotta admit it. That garden is beginnin' to look pretty good."

Slocum gave him three big, juicy tomatoes which he had concealed inside his shirt. Perkins looked around nervously. "The super don't like his tomatoes goin' anywhere 'cept his pocket," he whispered. He placed the tomatoes in his hat, which he then carried under his arm in a casual manner.

"So what?" Slocum said. "Want some cucumbers tomorrow? He'll never miss 'em."

Perkins grinned and nodded.

Next afternoon, Slocum remarked, as he handed four superb cucumbers to the guard, "I could use a couple candles. It gets pretty dark in the shack when the sun goes below the wall."

"Sure," Perkins said as he stuffed the cucumbers inside his jacket. He beckoned Slocum to follow. When he reached the storeroom he banged hard on the counter with his club.

Old Bob Tolliver jerked awake.

Perkins grinned. "Gotcha agin'," he said. Tolliver grunted.

"Give 'im two candles."

"An' matches," Slocum said.

"Yeah. Give 'im a box o' matches, Bob."

Tolliver handed them over. His hooded eyes were filled with hatred.

"The green onions're doin' fine," Slocum said. "Should be ready for pullin' tomorrow. How about a couple more candles?"

Perkins nodded. "Sure, why not?" he said. "Hey, three more candles, you old fart. An' be snappy!"

Tolliver handed them over silently.

"An' matches," Slocum prompted.

Perkins waved his hand. Tolliver handed Slocum three more boxes of matches.

He hoped the five candles would last for the entire construction of the tunnel. Slocum shoved them in his pockets.

"How's the cantaloupes?" Perkins asked.

"Got some nice ones comin' along. Should be ripe in a couple weeks."

"Good," Perkins said.

"I'll mark the best one fer you," Slocum said respectfully.

"Fine, just fine. Anythin' yuh want from the storeroom, you lemme know."

"Yes, sir," Slocum said respectfully. "It gets right hot out there. Wonder if we could have a couple canteens so's we don't have to keep comin' back here fer a drink."

"Sure thing," Perkins said, already dreaming of the fragrant orange flesh of ripe cantaloupes. They cost a dollar apiece in the markets in Yuma.

He turned and snapped out a harsh request for two canteens.

"Only s'posed to give 'em to guards on tower duty," Tolliver said.

"Give 'em to me or I'll wrap your guts 'round that stepladder," Perkins said.

A routine had been established. After breakfast the cook handed Slocum and Wagner two big sandwiches each. This was by Borden's orders. The superintendent was very pleased with the way Slocum had encouraged the garden to produce. The constant hoeing and spading, the digging into the soil of the chopped weeds, had resulted in healthy, high-yield plants.

Borden wanted the two gardeners to eat well. Healthy gardeners worked harder and, in the long run, made more money for him. And he did not have to pay personally for their food. It was marvelous, Borden thought. As for the canteens, Perkins thought he had better cover himself.

"I gave two canteens to them," he said. "Saved a lot of

time, else they'd be goin' back an' forth fer drinks all day long."

Borden agreed. "Sure," he said with approval.

But Slocum's real purpose in securing the canteens was his secret.

They would be needed for the desert crossing.

It gave him great pleasure to know that Borden was smiling at him as he walked through the garden with the canteens slung over his shoulder.

Late that afternoon, with four more feet excavated, he and Wagner were busily spading between the rows of corn.

"Shit," muttered Wagner. He lifted his spade to break up the lumps of clay which had just been dug out of the tunnel.

"What's the matter?" Slocum asked. He thought things were going well. The work of the last few days had sweated away Wagner's unhealthy fat; his flaccid muscles were getting stronger, and his hands were slowly developing callouses. He was learning physical endurance, a commodity which he would certainly need when they attempted to cross the Yuma and then the Lecheguilla Deserts.

"Goddamn clay!"

Slocum said, "Keep in mind that if we had to dig through sand, our tunnel would have come to a halt just as soon as it began."

"Don' follow you. How come?"

"Where would we get the lumber to support the roof?"

"Yeah," Wagner said after a few seconds. "Yeah. I see what yuh mean."

"An' notice, you're breathin' easier now. When you first started diggin' you sounded like a steam engine on an upgrade."

"Well, yeah," Wagner said. He felt a little proud of himself. Slocum never complimented him, but this was different.

They spaded in silence. The sun had gone down from its zenith, and both men were looking forward to washing in the river water that Slocum had pumped into the washtub. Slocum took off his shirt.

From her window overlooking the garden Judith Borden watched his back muscles bunch and knot as he dug and spaded. She began to breathe faster. She had to develop a plan to get Wagner out of the garden for an hour some day. She wanted to be alone with Slocum as soon as possible. She wanted to be screwed. The fact that she was, in a way, responsible for the existence of the garden — she had insisted that it be established three years before — made her the garden supervisor. No one would be suspicious if she should occasionally go down there on a tour of inspection. If her first visit should turn out to be a success, she intended to make her visits on a regular basis. She was a woman who demanded a lot sexually, and her husband could not fulfill her requirements.

The new prisoner was being well fed. He looked to be in excellent physical condition. She began thinking of how to get rid of Wagner for a few hours without arousing her husband's suspicion.

5

They had dug ten feet horizontally out toward the wall. The job, which had at first seemed very simple, had become complicated. Slocum had never dug an escape tunnel before.

First, there was no room to turn around and go back. A man went in head-first and flat on his stomach. He couldn't even crawl; he had to wiggle along like a snake. The lack of head space meant that he had to return feet-first.

The soil was clay: hard-packed clay. It had to be dug out chunk by chunk. This would not be much of a problem if a man had room to swing a pick, but there was no room.

Slocum solved the problem partly. He removed the pick from its handle. He swung the heavy pick like a dagger; this gouged out the tunnel face piece by piece.

The next problem was how to fill the sack. Then came the problem of how to remove the filled sack.

Slocum solved these by pushing the empty sack in front of him as he moved into the tunnel. As soon as he would excavate some more he would shove it into the sack with his free hand. But this, in turn, created still another problem: there was no room in the incredibly crammed space to fill a whole sack. So Slocum and Wagner found themselves forced to fill each sack to only one-third of its capacity.

Next the sack had to be tied up. The most ordinary movements become difficult in the cramped, airless space. Moreover, the heat of the burning candle drove the temperature up to an unbearable degree.

So thirst became a serious problem. There was no room to take a canteen along. They solved this situation by taking a long drink before they went down into the tunnel.

Frequently the candle would be knocked over and the flame would puff out. A man would reach for the box of friction matches and find out that the matches were saturated with sweat. They crumbled whenever they were scraped alongside the pick. When Slocum, who was the first to run across this problem, crawled out, he laid the damp matches next to the shack in the sun till they dried. They did so very quickly in the ferocious heat.

That taught them to remove the matches from their pockets as soon as the candle was lit.

When each man finished his last stint in the tunnel he crawled out. The washtub was set across the tunnel opening and a few empty sacks tossed casually alongside. The tub was filled with river water, warm and muddy. The sweat-soaked clothes were scrubbed. Then they were placed outside in the sun to dry. The ferocious heat dried them completely in five minutes. This action attracted no attention, since their clothes were saturated with sweat within five minutes of commencing their gardening work each morning.

Looking down at the drying clothes after the routine had been well established, Borden sent Perkins down with two bars of laundry soap.

"He said to tell you he likes the way you work," Perkins said grudgingly.

When he walked away, Slocum broke into muffled laughter.

"Jesus," Wagner said. Then he too started to laugh. It was the first time that Slocum had observed anything more than a sneer or a cynical expression on Wagner's face.

Slocum was pleased. It was a relief to see Wagner smiling for a change. Both of them had a hard road ahead. Putting aside the literal meaning of the phrase: the digging, the brutal trip across the desert and the dry, inhospitable cañons, the roaming Yaquis and Apaches who killed any helpless traveller, they also faced the horrible psychological weight of being in a tunnel.

For the first few feet there was no problem. Whoever would be working there had light pouring in from the opening. But as the tunnel continued the daylight would vanish. Then the more menacing darkness began.

Yet this was bearable. What made it nerve-wracking was the constant possibility that the tunnel roof would collapse. Slocum put this thought away. He hoped that Wagner would not suddenly think of it, especially when he was working at the tunnel face.

A tunnel blocked, no way to crawl out, a rapidly lessening supply of air. The thought of choking to death in the darkness, in a space so cramped that a man could not even turn around, was enough to make even a brave man fearful.

When the tunnel was only four feet away from the base of the wall, Mrs. Borden solved her problem.

She casually remarked at dinner that it was time to repaint their living quarters.

"We had it painted only two years ago, Judith."

"I'm aware of that," she said coldly. "I did not choose

this horrible green shade. I want to change it to a pale yellow."

"But—"

"This place is awful enough without my having to look at that depressing color every day. And it's not as if you have to pay for the labor."

That was true. The prisoners did all of the work in their quarters.

So Borden yielded. She went next morning to Mc-Teague's General Emporium and bought five gallons of pale yellow paint and the necessary thinner and brushes. It was delivered that afternoon. By then she had asked Perkins to send a couple of prisoners who could handle furniture without breaking it. They had shifted the furniture from the drawing room into the hallway. They next washed the walls. She dismissed one of them and asked the other man to stay behind to do the painting. He was close to sixty and had lost most of his teeth. He was also clumsy, something which she had noticed when he was shifting the furniture.

She watched him as he began to paint. Satisfied, she walked into Borden's office.

"Yes, Judith?" He spoke abruptly. Perkins was standing beside Borden's desk holding a sheaf of papers.

"That man," she began.

"What about him? Perkins says he's quiet an' well-behaved. Is there any trouble?"

"No. But he *smells.*"

"Oh, for God's sake!"

"I don't want anyone who smells in my house!"

Perkins suppressed a grin.

"Judith—"

"How about one of those gardeners? They take a bath every day and they wash their clothes too."

Borden thought. The big one did most of the gardening work. Let her have the smaller man.

"All right," he said. To Perkins he said, "Tell Wagner he'll be paintin' my quarters tomorrow."

"Thanks," she said.

"And it's a good time for me to do some business," he told her. "I can't stand the smell of paint. I might as well ride down to Somerton and talk to Charlie Bear." Charlie Bear was a sub-chief of the Yumas. He lived in a brush hut in Somerton, about twenty miles south of Yuma. Borden prided himself on his astuteness. He planned to tell Charlie that the prison was still giving fifty-dollar rewards for any escaped prisoners the Yumas brought back. Besides, to seal the agreement, the Yuma chief was in the habit of letting Borden screw one of his young daughters. Borden handed the chief a bottle of cheap whiskey. Charlie called in one of the girls, and then went to drink it under a dense stand of cottonwoods that grew along a narrow creek that emptied into the Colorado.

Borden watched his wife walk away. She hadn't been so friendly for a long time. Later that night, thinking about the daughter of Charlie Bear he was going to screw tomorrow, and aroused by the thought, he put a hand on her breast.

She pushed it away and mumbled, "Too tired."

She smiled secretly. If she would have asked right away for Prendergast, her husband would have been suspicious. This way, Borden himself had made the suggestion. And now she would try the new man with little chance of discovery, especially since Borden would be away most of the day. She squeezed her thighs together in anticipation and shuddered.

Early next morning, after Borden had ridden out, she said,

"I want you to do a good, careful job."

"Yes'm," Wagner said in his usual sullen fashion.

"Or you'll have to do it all over again."

"Yes'm." He tried to keep the rage out of his face and voice. There would be no work on the tunnel as long as he was stuck painting in the bitch's quarters. Only if one of them was on watch could the other man work in the tunnel. It was going better than he had dreamed of when they started. He thought of Slocum with grudging respect.

He picked up the sponge, dipped it into the soapy water, and began to scrub the walls.

"Be sure you wipe off all that soapy water."

"Yes'm."

"Take as long as you need for the job," she said. "There's no rush."

"Yes'm," Wagner said, hating her.

Sitting at her bureau, she put on a broad-brimmed straw hat. She put on a touch of rouge. She got up, walked through her apartment, across a corridor, and down the steps into the garden. It was noon. The white, intense glare of the sun was so strong that no one was asked to work during this time. The gardener was sure to be taking his siesta. She moved slowly through the rows of tomatoes. The soil had been well-spaded; no weeds were visible, and neatly edged channels for the river water ran beside each row of plants. She pretended to observe everything to see how they were coming along. One never knew if someone might be watching. The possibility of discovery made it exciting for her; life in Yuma was boring beyond belief. She moved closer to the shack.

Slocum had pumped the washtub full of water. It was slightly muddy, but that was never a problem, especially after the morning's session with the hoe. Hoeing made the dust spurt up and settle on his bare, sweat-soaked skin. Any kind of water was a delight after that. After he had scrubbed himself and washed off the soapsuds he liked to lie back and plan his next step. He was wondering how they would be able to get hold of some guns for the desert crossing, a serious problem since they would be escaping without any money, when Mrs. Borden walked into the shack.

He was leaning back in the tub with his arms along the edges. She thought that he looked like a king on his throne. She said nothing. She stared at his thickly muscled arms, the broad shoulders, the hard, flat planes of his stomach, so different from the ugly little pot belly of her husband. There were knife scars on his arms and shoulders; some grizzly-claw marks had put four parellel scars just below his rib cage on the right side.

Without a word she removed her hat and looked around. A wooden peg stuck out from the wall near him. She hung her hat on it. The movement brought her closer. She looked down at him. She stared at his penis in the soapy water. He did not move, but her closeness excited him. He had not slept with a woman in the past three months. His penis, engorged with blood, stood erect. She stared at it as it elevated itself above the black, curly pubic hair.

A long white scar ran across his lower back. Her eyes roamed over his body. She pointed to it.

"Sabre cut," he said, "Chickamauga."

"Stand up," she said hoarsely. "I want to dry you."

Slocum didn't move.

"Mr. Borden will be away all day. Perkins went with him. No one else will come into the garden." That was true; in order to prevent anyone else taking any expensive vegetables, Borden had put the garden off limits to everyone.

"Stand up!" she said once more.

This time he stood up. She began to rub him with the old flour sack that served as a towel. He reached out and unbuttoned her blouse. Her big firm breasts jiggled as she wiped his chest and shoulders. His penis stiffened. Sweat began to shine on her face.

"Turn around," she said thickly. Slocum turned around. She dried his back. "Step out of the tub," she said. He obeyed. She kneeled behind him and reached between his thighs. She grabbed his penis and ran her fingertips along its length. She gently cupped his testicles in her left palm and continued to stroke his penis.

He turned. She pressed her face against his groin and licked her lips till they were wet. Then she slid them back and forth against his penis while she cupped his balls in her palms and gently squeezed them.

She looked up at his face while she slid her mouth over the head of his penis. He let out a long sigh of pleasure. She ran her hot, wet mouth down the length of his shaft while her tongue flicked in and out. When she sensed that he was about to ejaculate, she lessened the intensity of her sucking. He managed to control himself. Then she lowered her head and began to run her tongue up and down.

He reached down and pulled off her blouse. She helped by shrugging her shoulders till the blouse slid off. He reached down and cupped a heavy, firm breast in each palm. The hard nipples jutted into his palms. When she felt his callouses scratch against her nipples she shuddered. Her breath began to come faster. She rocked from side to side, forcing her nipples against the rough skin.

She pulled up her skirt till it reached her hips. Underneath, she was naked except for her buttoned black shoes. Slocum went to his knees. He put a hand between her full, white thighs. He ran a forefinger along the inner surface of her vulva. It was soaking wet. At the top, the clitoris was swollen erect for its entire length.

Slocum moistened his forefinger and stroked the clitoris. She pressed hard against his finger and started to grind her hips. Her mouth began to slide up and down his penis while she moaned in anticipation. Once more he felt on the verge of exploding. She sucked the few drops of fluid that started to ooze from the end of his penis. Suddenly she stood up, pulled her dress over her head, and kicked a few sacks together. She lay back on them and opened her legs wide. She lifted them high. Her juices made her thighs glisten in the dim light that filtered into the shack.

"Now!" she gasped, with harsh intensity. *"Now!"*

Slocum kneeled. His penis slid in. Although she had lubricated in anticipation, she was tight. She obviously had not been screwed for some time. Ordinarily he would have tried to prolong it, but it would not be safe to do that here.

He plunged in all the way. She let out a half-pained, half-ecstatic gasp.

"Oh yes!" she cried. "More! *Harder!*"

She locked her ankles around Slocum's back. He thrust once more as hard as he could. The power of his drive forced her to slide four inches along the floor. She moaned with pleasure.

He bent his head and sucked her right nipple. His hips worked like pistons, driving in the hard steel of his inflamed penis. She grabbed the back of his head and forced her nipple even deeper into his mouth.

"Do that! Do that too!"

Slocum drove into her deeper and harder. The force of his drive pushed her against the washtub.

"Don't stop! Don't you dare stop!"

Her vagina began to squeeze and release, squeeze and release. Slocum could not hold back any more. His sperm shot up deep inside just as her orgasm swept over her. She put a finger in her mouth and bit it as hard as she could to prevent herself from screaming. Each time his penis throbbed, her legs tightened convulsively against his back.

Finally he was finished. He let out a long breath and lay motionless. Both their naked bodies were slick with sweat. She wriggled sensuously underneath. The sweat was like oil; she was like a slippery eel.

He pulled out and began to dress. If someone were to see them, he hated to think what might happen. He handed her her skirt. She sat up and smiled and held up her arms. He pulled her to her feet. She moved against him and rubbed her naked breasts against his chest.

"Oh, my," she said softly. "Oh, my."

He held the skirt above her head. She held her arms straight up. At that second he noticed that their passionate lovemaking had dislodged the washtub. In her line of sight was the open shaft to the escape tunnel.

He immediately turned her around so that she faced the other direction. He pulled her skirt into place. Then he stepped up behind her. He cupped her breasts in his hands and gently squeezed her nipples. Her head fell back against his chest. She closed her eyes.

"That feels so good," she whispered. With his left foot, Slocum pushed the washtub back into place. She had not noticed anything out of place. She began to rub her buttocks against his groin in a sensuous circular movement. His penis grew hard. Suddenly she pulled away and said briskly, as she reached for her blouse, "That's so you will remember me."

She turned and walked out, putting on her hat at the door.

She left without a backward glance. Slocum grinned. He pumped water into the washtub, got into it once more, and then she suddenly appeared at the door.

"I'll be back," she said, with a cool smile. "I like the way you take care of my garden." She turned and was gone.

She was good, Slocum thought, and would probably do much better on a comfortable bed. But trouble would follow this woman, of that he was sure. Besides, she would only come when Wagner was not there. And if Wagner was not there, how could work proceed on the tunnel?

6

Wagner cleaned the walls quickly and more efficiently than he had ever done anything in his life. He was in a fever of impatience to get back to the tunnel. The walls dried within minutes because of the dry heat. He began immediately to stir the paint. Mrs. Borden returned, gave the walls a cursory glance, and watched Wagner narrowly. She had hoped that he would have done a bad or sloppy job which would then need re-doing.

But he had performed his task faultlessly. She realized then that it would be somewhat difficult to arrange another meeting with the tall man with the green eyes. She shuddered with anticipation at the thought. But she was confident of her ability to seize the opportunity when it came. Next time she planned to sit astride him as he sat on the bench. She would ride him like a horse. She felt dizzy with pleasure at the thought of how deeply he would drive into her.

*   *   *

It happened without warning the next day.

A section of the roof suddenly collapsed behind Slocum as he lay flat on his belly swinging the pick. When it fell with a heavy *thump!* he turned his head. The collapse had filled the tunnel from floor to roof.

The first thing he did was to blow out the candle. He had to conserve oxygen while he planned his next move. He fought against his instinct to yell for help. It would waste air and no yell could penetrate the clay. Besides, Wagner would be sitting in the doorway, several feet from the shaft opening. Flat on his face, he could feel his heart beating wildly like a triphammer. He forced himself to be calm. Panic would kill him. Decisions made in an hysterically impulsive manner would waste valuable time and breath.

Yelling would do no good. He examined that thought once more. No. No good. The thought came suddenly to him that, with the tunnel collapse in back of him and the tunnel face in front of him, he was in something very uncomfortably like a coffin. His only hope, he realized, was that Wagner might sense that something was wrong and come down to investigate. Then he thought, *Wagner will think that I'm doing so well down there that I want to extend my shift time*. And that would just be hunky-dory with Wagner. He hated it in the tunnel and would be delighted that Slocum wanted to stay below some more.

"Shit," Slocum muttered with feeling. He had to attract Wagner's attention some way or other, before his oxygen ran out. He considered.

He pulled up both legs as close to his chest that he could. Then he snapped out both his heavy shoe soles as hard as he could against the wall of fallen clay. It made a faint thumping sound.

He repeated the kick four times, with ten seconds between each attempt. After the last kick he noticed that his lungs were beginning to pump hard in an involuntary attempt to get more oxygen. Each time he had pulled back his legs and drove them at the wall he used up more air. He knew that if he remained still he would have more air to live on until Wagner might check out the tunnel.

But if he didn't try to attract Wagner's attention—and if Wagner did not come to investigate—then Slocum would surely die.

It was a dilemma. And the only solution that had a chance was for Slocum to use up the available air by kicking at the wall.

He kicked again. His lungs now felt as if a broad, white-hot iron band had been clamped on his chest; and now it was slowly being tightened with a screw device. He felt that he was choking. He knew he could only kick a few more times before he would begin to thrash around and gasp like a trout that had just been caught by a fisherman and flung ashore. He hoped he would have courage enough not to scream when the end came.

Wagner was idly scraping away with the file. He was putting a sharp edge on a hoe. It was windless and hot, as usual, and he was dripping with sweat even though he was sitting in the shade. He got up to take a drink of water from the canteen that hung on a wall peg. His route to the canteen took him past the shaft opening. He tilted the canteen back and drank the water, which was kept cool by the evaporation from the damp canvas covering.

As he turned to put the canteen back he heard a very faint thumping noise. It meant nothing to him. The sound meant nothing. The thought of going into the tunnel to see what it was did not occur to him. After all, if he went down into the tunnel, what would happen to their venture if Perkins should suddenly take it into his head to make a surprise visit? Who would be up there to shove the washtub into place over the shaft opening?

The violent kicks loosened more of the tunnel roof. With a sudden rumble, two more feet of the tunnel roof collapsed.

Wagner heard the nose as he was hanging up the canteen. This awakened his curiosity. He leaned into the shaft and said, "John." There was no answer. He realized something was wrong. He took a hurried glance into the garden, did not see any guard, and then he slid down head-first into the tunnel. When he realized that there was no light in the tunnel he knew something was wrong.

This time he yelled. "John!"

Very faintly he heard a whistle in response. He crawled ahead till he bumped head-first into the collapsed segment. Then he knew immediately what must have happened. He had warned Slocum that this might happen, and it did. Cursing, he slid backward, stood up in the vertical shaft, and grabbed an empty sack. He pushed it in front of him back into the tunnel, filled it, tugged it out, and emptied it. He went down again and filled it. He wrestled it out, emptied it, and went down again, always filled with the fear that Perkins might make a surprise visit and find out everything. Escape attempts were rewarded with an additional five-year sentence.

He went down again, praying that no one would come by.

On the other side of the fall, Slocum heard the scraping noises as Wagner grabbed and heaved the clay lumps into the sack. There was nothing he could do to help. He felt that Wagner was turning out much better than he had thought. Slocum lay inert, conserving the little air remaining.

Wagner was drenched with sweat. He went down again. He was exhausted with the unaccustomed burst of energy. What kept him going was his anger at Slocum, who had refused his advice that they build props for the tunnel roof as they proceeded. Wagner's anger infused his body with energy.

Slocum was rapidly depleting the little oxygen remaining. He was breathing almost pure carbon dioxide now. He felt dizzy. He began to pant like a dog in hot, windless weather.

Just before Wagner finished filling the fifth sack, he pulled a thirty-pound lump of clay from the top of the pile. Air flowed suddenly through the gap. Slocum took a long, deep, gasping breath of fresh air. He thought, *Now the stupid son of a bitch just saved my life.*

It took two hours to spade in the clay from the collapsed tunnel.

Slocum had long ago learned that supervisors of any kind—sergeants, lieutenants, ranch foremen, and even prison guards—always relaxed their innate suspicion whenever they saw people moving with something in their hands. It meant they were working and not fucking off.

So he was not worried about what Borden or Perkins would make of the bushels full of clay that were being carried to all parts of the garden. They would see purposeful movement. That would satisfy them. If they were to pause to think about it, they would come to the conclusion that it must have something to do with the improvement of the garden.

When they had finished and were sitting panting in the shade, drenched with sweat, Perkins suddenly appeared. He reached out and slammed his club against Slocum's soles.

"I said, 'stand up,' you son of a bitch!"

Slocum stood up slowly. His face was impassive as he fought to control himself. Any response that Perkins didn't like would be rewarded with a stay in the snake den, manacled to the stone floor.

"You think you c'n git away with fuckin' off 'cause you ain't got me hangin' over you? I'm here to tell you you can't! The super's comin'. Look sharp, or you'll be sorry you was ever born."

Borden appeared in the doorway. "You're yellin' pretty loud there," he observed.

"They was sleepin'."

"We—" Wagner began in an injured tone. Slocum kicked him in the ankle.

"They look too sweaty for sleepin'," Borden remarked.

"Bet they was screwin' each other up the ass," Perkins said with a broad grin.

Slocum put a warning hand on Wagner's arm. They were too close to finishing the tunnel to risk being sent off to the snake den.

"Sir," he said, "we're takin' goddamn good care of the goddamn garden."

Borden turned around. He looked up and down the neatly spaded rows. Not a weed was in sight. Water was slowly flowing down the narrow irrigation ditches and soaking into the roots of each plant. Full ripe tomatoes, big as Slocum's two hands together, were hanging among the thick green leaves.

"I never saw the garden look so good, Perkins. That don't look like they're fuckin' off, does it, now? Every time

I take a look out the window they're either spadin' or hoein'. They're real sunburnt. If they take themselves a siesta when the sun's right overhead, I got no complaints."

Perkins was silent.

"Well, Perkins?"

Perkins growled, "Don' trust 'em."

"Why?"

"Jus' don', is all." He slapped his club against his meaty palm and glowered.

Slocum's smile infuriated him. He took half a step toward Slocum and lifted his club.

"Perkins!"

The guard stopped grudgingly.

"I see 'em workin' all the time, Perkins. *All* the time. Every time I look out the window I see 'em spadin' or hoein'. Men like that deserve a little break. I'm goin' to see they get it. That clear?" He turned toward Slocum. "The garden's doin' real fine. You been workin' real hard. Take it easy a while. Take yourselves a long siesta."

Slocum smiled. The longer the siesta, the more time they could spend on the tunnel. Perkins noticed the smile. His face darkened with suppressed rage. There was something in that smile he could not quite understand. It made him feel uneasy and annoyed.

"Thanks," Slocum said.

Borden turned and left. Perkins lingered. "Wipe that smile off your face," he muttered, "or I'll wipe it off with this." He lifted his club and smacked it against his palm.

"Yes, sir," Slocum said cheerfully. His face was impassive.

That decision of Borden's gave them more time to work on the tunnel. When they finished their digging that afternoon,

Slocum pushed a sharpened stake through the roof of the tunnel. When it hit rock and splintered, he knew that they were under the exterior wall. Three more feet would be sure to put them outside the wall. Then an upward slant of four feet or so would let them emerge to freedom.

The problem then would be how to get out without being seen.

This was serious. They would not be able to emerge from their completed tunnel at night. Every day at five, Perkins arrived to herd them back to their cells.

Getting out by day would take extraordinary luck.

Unless Slocum could arrange a diversion. He would think about that.

Two days later, they had two more feet to go. Slocum was in the tunnel. Suddenly he heard the double tap on the hoe that meant someone was coming. He snaked backward so quickly that his knees were scraped raw. He had just enough time to hoist himself out of the shaft and shove the washtub into place when Perkins arrived. Wagner walked in with him, talking.

He stared at Slocum, who was dirty and drenched with sweat.

Perkins said, "Don't you guys ever stop workin'?"

Slocum was pleased with the question. It was clear that no one suspected the existence of the tunnel. And it was clear as well that Wagner, after he had given the alarm, had walked out of the shack, met Perkins, and engaged him in conversation for a few seconds, which gave Slocum just enough time to conceal the shaft opening. Slocum observed Wagner looking at the washtub, then he let out a relieved sigh.

The kid was improving.

"Time passes faster when we work," Slocum said.

Perkins grunted. "Yeah. I s'pose. Wagner, Miz Borden wants you up at the apartment."

"Shit," Wagner muttered.

"'Shit'? Man, you got to be the only man in Yuma who'd say *that*. I'd like to find her shoes under my bed. But don' try to grab some o' that. Borden ain't gonna like it."

"Why she want me?" Wagner asked impatiently.

"Says you din't do such a good job on her walls. Says when the paint dried she found a lot of holidays all over. She got paint and a brush waitin' fer you. Get movin'."

Wagner hung up the hoe he had been working on. He walked through the garden, trailed by Perkins, who turned his head once to stare at Slocum. He was puzzled. He had figured the man for a troublemaker, but the man was working harder than any previous gardener ever had. It was a mystery to Perkins, who usually prided himself on his ability to predict the behavior of the new convicts.

He had guessed wrong on this one, he decided.

Earlier that morning Borden had told his wife that he would be riding upriver to the agency for the Colorado River tribes. He planned to talk to the chiefs in the presence of the agent. His purpose was to lock the barn door before the horses were stolen.

"I don't know what you're talking about. Horses?"

"No, not horses. What I meant was—"

"Can't you talk plainly?"

"I thought it was obvious," he said with annoyance. "Anyone goes and breaks out of Yuma, I'll have him picked in case he heads north along the river. He's got to stick close to the river or he'll die of thirst. I think that's pretty smart."

"Yes," she said with a bored expression. "Real smart."

"I'll be gone all day," he said. "Prob'ly get back after dark." As he turned to pick up his wallet from the marble bureau top, he saw her reflection in the mirror that hung over the bureau. Her face looked delighted. But the expression vanished very quickly, to be replaced by one of boredom, as soon as she realized that he was looking at her.

It was then that Borden thought it would be a good idea to return unexpectedly, long before she thought he might be back.

"I'm not satisfied with the paint job that man Wagner did," she said with studied casualness.

Borden shoved his wallet into his coat pocket. He unhooked his gunbelt from the clothes tree and buckled it on. The paint job had looked fine to him. He was silent. Let her dig herself in.

"Why?"

"It looks too thin in lots of places," she said.

"I'll tell Perkins to get 'im up here," Borden said. In the mirror her face showed hastily concealed delight.

Was she screwing Wagner? It would be easy to find out, he considered.

"When did you say you'd be back?"

"About six or seven, I reckon."

"I'll hold dinner."

"Sure."

He decided to be back about two.

The affair would be childishly easy to discover. He rode along Gila Street, hitched his horse in the rear of Hell's Half Acre, and went in through the back door, which is what most of Yuma's respectable businessmen did when they didn't want their wives to know where they were, and spent two hours playing poker. At the end of that time he stood up. He was a bit unsteady on his feet. He had been drinking rye steadily. Leaving his horse still behind the saloon, he walked along Gila Street till he reached the prison. The man on duty in the main guard tower had seen him coming up Gila Street. He yelled down to the guard at the gate.

It swung open at his approach and he walked inside the yard. He was so angry as he imagined what his wife was doing with Wagner that he did not respond to the guard's salute. He walked quickly across the yard. As soon as he reached the steps that led to his apartment he slowed down and looked up at the tower. No one was looking at him. Good; he hated the idea of anyone up there finding out what was going on.

He pulled off his boots and stood in his stocking feet. Holding the boots in his right hand, he went up the stairs slowly. He held on to the banister with his left hand in order to take the weight off his feet and lessen the creaking noise made on the dry and warped treads. When he reached the door to his apartment he paused, and looked down the stairs to make sure that none of the guards were watching. He ripped the door open and raced into the bedroom.

The only one inside it was Wagner. He was yawning as he finished the brush stroke. He turned with a startled expression and stared at Borden. Borden was staring at the bed. There were no signs of recent activity on it. It was neatly made up.

"Lookin' for Mrs. Borden," he snapped. He was suddenly aware that he was carrying his boots in his hand.

"Went out 'bout half an hour ago," Wagner said. He dipped his brush into the paint pail.

"Say where she was goin'?" Borden sat in a chair and pulled on his boots.

Wagner's face showed curiosity. "Nope."

"What did you an' her talk about?"

"Huh?" Wagner said, with a look of genuine puzzlement. Borden decided that no one could be such a good actor.

"Nemmin'. Get back to work." He debated what to do next. Perhaps he was wrong to be suspicious? He stood up. He decided to look at the garden. The sight of the superb vegetables growing so nicely—and on which he was making an excellent profit in the Yuma market—always soothed him. Maybe she had gone shopping. In that case, he had nothing to worry about.

She sat astride Slocum. Her body sucked and squeezed his penis like a wet, powerful mouth. She rose and fell, rose and fell. His hands slid under her white buttocks—her dress was pulled up to her armpits—and helped lift her with each rise.

She began to let out long, whimpering moans that increased in volume as she neared orgasm. She bent down her head and, thrusting her tongue into Slocum's mouth, she sucked his tongue. As her excitement rose, she pulled her head away, bent down, and bit his shoulder in an attempt to stifle her moans. Her hips writhed and twisted around his cock like a snake that had been pinned down under a forked branch.

In spite of her determination to be quiet, she could not control herself. A long moan escaped. Slocum clapped his hand across her mouth. She was whimpering and moaning so loudly that he did not hear Borden's stealthy approach. The gesture was useless. Above her shoulder, Slocum suddenly saw Borden staring at them.

7

Borden was speechless. So this was the reason why she wanted the place repainted! To give her a chance to be alone with Prendergast!

Slocum watched Borden narrowly. The man's shaking hand dropped to his gun butt. His wife was still astride Slocum. Borden was ten feet away and standing in the doorway.

Borden could kill both of them easily at that distance. The Colt came out and wavered between the two of them.

Slocum said calmly, "Get off." She sat up, and then slowly dismounted. She let her skirt fall to her ankles. One hand went up and rearranged her dishevelled hair. Borden's face was white. Her calm nonchalance was enraging to her husband. His face looked drained.

"You—" he began. "You—" he began again, but his throat was so constricted that words could not escape. Slocum could see that the man was on the verge of murder.

"You can kill us," Slocum said calmly. "And then your troubles will begin." As he had guessed, this stopped Borden for a moment.

"What troubles?" he yelled.

"They can hear you," Slocum said, as he jerked his head toward the prison, visible through the open doorway of the shack.

Borden's voice automatically dropped. "How long has this been goin' on?" he demanded of his wife.

"It's goin' to be very embarrassin'," Slocum said.

"What the hell are you talkin' about?" Borden said, his voice strangled with hatred.

"To explain it," Slocum said patiently. He stood up and buttoned his fly. "Since it's gonna be obvious what was goin' on in here. No way that it can be kept a secret. People're gonna smile when you go by. In the prison and on the streets of Yuma. I can promise you that."

Borden tried to think of something to say, but part of him knew that the man was right. In a little town like Yuma, everyone knew everything about everyone else.

"And I can prevent it."

The calm tone had its effect on Borden. It both enraged and intrigued him. Slocum sensed his hesitation and prepared to work on it.

"You got a goddamn nerve!"

"All you have to do," Slocum continued, "is not say a word. I'll keep my mouth shut, and so will Mrs. Borden. You can be sure of that. You could've killed her just now. The fact that you didn't will make her damn sure to watch her step from now on."

She watched him in amazement. Slocum turned to her and said, "A .45 slug can punch a hole in you big as my fist." Her eyes widened. She looked scared. Slocum was pleased with the effect of his graphic description.

"If we all keep quiet about this," he went on, "you'll hold your job. If you kill us, you'll be dropped as superintendent like a red-hot coal. You might even wind up in here as a convict. Juries are funny."

The muzzle of the .45 wavered.

"If you'll send Wagner back here," Slocum said, seizing the initiative, "we'll get back to work. We've got more irrigation and hoein' to do. We're goin' to get a big tomato crop real soon."

She could not take her eyes from him. Talking calmly about tomatoes when her husband wanted to kill him!

But Slocum had calculated his man correctly. The passion and greed for money, the security of the job as Superintendent—which Borden had received because he had helped get out the vote for the successful candidate for senator—and the desire to avoid public contempt as a cuckolded husband whose wife was being screwed by a convict—all of these motivations held Borden back from pulling the trigger.

"Get upstairs!" he said to his wife.

She turned and walked out without a word.

Borden holstered the Colt slowly. He looked at Slocum for a few seconds. Hatred oozed out of him like a corrosive acid. Then he turned on his heels and walked away.

"I don't know what the hell's eatin' Borden," Wagner complained. "He come stormin' in while I was paintin' an' tol' me to get the hell back down here. I said I wasn't finished, an' he yelled 'Get the fuck down there!' And Miz Borden, she didn't say a single goddamn word. I allus thought she wore the pants up there."

"Not today. Wagner, you an' I are gonna start workin' real hard from now on. Real *hard*."

"Shit, John, we're workin' real hard right now."

"Not hard enough."

"But—"

Slocum held up his hand. He told Wagner what had just happened.

Wagner's mouth fell open. "You mean you was gettin' screwed when I was paintin'?"

"Only twice, Wagner. Only twice."

"That's twice more'n what I got. Jesus! You—"

"Borden's now figurin' how he can kill me in a legal way. In a couple days or so, he'll come up with an answer. So we'll only have two more days to finish up here. That's it. *Comprende?*"

"What d'ya mean, a nice legal way?"

"Shot while attemptin' to escape. What's wrong with that?"

"Oh, shit," Wagner muttered. "You mean if he sees that tunnel all he has to do is shoot us? That's how he'll handle it?"

"Yep. So we might as well give him a real good tunnel. I'm goin' down right now. You see anyone comin', just bang on the hoe.

"But it ain't our lunch hour! That's risky!"

Slocum looked at him. Wagner dropped his eyes, muttered under his breath, grabbed a hoe, and, walking outside, began to hoe. As soon as Wagner was out the door, Slocum pulled the washtub aside.

When he reached the face of the tunnel, he ran into luck, because he found that the clay was now mixed with sand. The work went much faster. In half an hour he was pulling pure sand backward. There was no longer any need to use the pick. His hands were tools enough. He backed out and slid in again with an empty sack.

He made six trips dragging out the full sacks. The backs of his fingers were scraped raw. He dumped the sand in back of the shack. It was Wagner's turn to go down. Slocum began to hoe in his turn, and to work the sand into the garden. An hour passed. Slocum moved into the shack for a drink of water from the canteen. While he drank, standing in the doorway, he could see Borden's face glowering at him from the window of his apartment. They had better escape fast.

When he was about to walk back to his hoe Wagner's wild, jubilant face emerged from the shaft.

"Light, light!" he whispered. "Light!" He stepped out of the shaft and hugged Slocum. "I saw light!"

"Slow down! What happened?"

"I was pullin' the sand back. It's real easy now. An' suddenly I pull my hand back with sand, you know, and there's light. An' a draft shoots in an' blows out the candle! We're through!"

Slocum's ears were sharp, but because of Wagner's excited babbling he did not hear Perkins's stealthy approach. The guard took in the scene: Wagner, covered with sand and sweat; the open shaft, and, most damning of all, Wagner's excited announcement.

As Perkins turned to yell for help, Slocum rammed the end of his hoe into Perkins' solar plexus. Temporarily paralyzed, the guard let out a loud grunt of pain and surprise and bent over in a crouch, both hands on his stomach. Slocum tripped him and sent him sprawling headlong into the shack. No longer could he be seen from the prison windows. He caught his breath and was about to yell when Slocum dropped on his chest with both knees. Perkins's breath went out with a loud, explosive grunt.

Wagner was standing, rigid with surprise.

Slocum held a palm over the guard's mouth. "Quick!" Slocum said. "Tie him!"

Wagner looked around wildly and said, "With what?"

"For Christ's sake! Use his shirt!"

Wagner tore Perkins's shirt into strips and tied the man's wrists together. He did a decent job, Slocum saw. "Now the feet!" Slocum snapped. "Come on, man!"

Wagner gave him a resentful look, but finished the job. "Two more strips!"

Slocum shoved one strip into Perkins's mouth. The other he used to hold the gag fast in place.

He turned to Wagner. "We leave right now."

"In *daylight?*"

Slocum paid no attention to the panicky incredulous tone.

"Go to Perkins's room. If someone sees you say that Borden sent you to get 'im. Pull all the beddin' onto the floor. Dump the kerosene from the lamps all over the beddin'. Drop a match on it an' get back here. Take some tomatoes with you, as if you're bringin' some up to Perkins's room. No one'll look at you twice. I'll be in the tunnel. Soon's you get back here, pull the washtub in after you and drag it with you. Got that?"

"What the hell do you want the washtub for?"

"So help me God," Slocum said, "I'll kill you if you don't do just what I say! This is our only chance. Don't fuck up."

"But—"

"Shut up! Go!"

Wagner gave one last despairing look at Slocum before he left. Slocum stared down for a couple of seconds at Perkins, who looked up at him with hatred.

"You oughta be glad I didn't kill you, you prick," Slocum said conversationally. He unhooked the two canteens from their wall pegs and slid into the shaft.

At the end of the tunnel there was a bright hole at the face as big as a dime. Slocum pulled away with both hands. The sand was heavily compacted, but it broke off in fist-sized chunks as he tugged away. He broke them up with his fist. Next he spread the sand evenly all over the floor of the tunnel; this time it would not be necessary to haul it out.

By this time, Wagner had dragged the washtub along the tunnel. Slocum had widened the opening so that it was wide enough for them to crawl through and take the washtub with them. The opening was on the precipitous bank of the Colorado, eight feet above the smooth brown flow of the river. Across the river there were no structures, no adobe houses, no stables. The current was running swiftly. Slocum guessed that it was doing about three knots, as fast as a man could walk.

As they waded into the river Slocum turned back for a quick look at the prison. Thick black smoke poured into the sky, driven eastward by the wind. They could hear the faint yells of the guards as they tried to organize a bucket brigade among the prisoners.

Slocum tugged the washtub out of the tunnel. They could not be seen from above, since they were at the foot of the wall. The guards in the tower could not see them from this angle.

"Jesus!" Wagner cried. "We're out! We're out!"

Across the river a line of adobe huts stretched along the shore. Children played in the shallows. "Don't keep lookin' around, for Christ's sake," Slocum said with some sharpness.

"We goin' to ride in *that?*" demanded Wagner.

"Get in the water."

Slocum had slung the canteens over his shoulders. They waded in up to their shoulders. The kids across the river stopped their splashing and screaming and watched the two men. Slocum turned the washtub upside down. He waved at the children and they waved back.

"What the hell didja do that for?"

"They'll think we're playin', same as they are. Duck under."

The air trapped inside the washtub kept it afloat. "Jesus, you want me to get under that?"

"Yes! And now!"

Wagner obeyed. Once underneath, holding the washtub by its edge, they kicked themselves out into the current. The children began to scream with excitement. They splashed along in the shallows trying to keep pace, but the current was too fast. The sound of the yelling diminished and then disappeared. Bored, the children went back to their old game.

The washtub floated south. Slocum let the current take them. He was tense. He had not counted on being seen by the children, and there was a good chance that the excitement of the children might have been noticed by someone in the main guard tower.

He was right. The guards up there turned their attention away from the smoke pouring from the windows. They saw the children waving and pointing at what was only a washtub.

"Stupid fuckin' kids," one guard grunted. "They want us to fetch 'em that old tub!"

"Can't blame 'em," the other one said. "It's worth a few bucks and those Mex kids're real poor."

"Keep your eye on the yard!" the other guard said. "But my wife would like that tub herself. Now some Yuma squaw downriver is gonna get it." He lifted his rifle and aimed it at the tub.

"Hold it!"

"Hell, if my wife can't get it, no one will."

The other guard knocked the rifle up. "Borden hears that shot, he'll have your ass."

"Yeah. All right." The guard grudgingly dropped the barrel.

Now they were past the cluster of adobe houses. The current moved steadily south. Within fifteen minutes, after the excitement of the fire had died down, Slocum was sure that Perkins's disappearance would be noticed. Someone would go looking for him. They'd find him and then realize that two prisoners had escaped via the tunnel to the river.

Then the guards in the tower would recall the kids' excitement. The chase would begin. Slocum figured they had very little time to get ashore and find a good hiding place. He ducked under, and risked a quick look at the shore.

They had drifted a mile and a half past the prison on its bluff. It was now out of sight around a bend. On the eastern shore was a marsh.

"Let's head for that," Slocum said. "Kick!"

He had noticed a dense stand of willows on the river edge of the marsh. They could get ashore there without being noticed.

The washtub bumped against the willow trunks. Slocum held on to the washtub with one hand while he ducked under and came up under the willow branches. No one was in sight. He reached under and tugged at Wagner's leg. Wagner came up sputtering.

Reeds grew thickly along the shore. Slocum parted them and looked upriver. Smoke still curled lazily above the prison. The brown river flowed placidly south. There were no signs of pursuit. He shoved hard at the washtub. It spurted five feet into the river and then moved majestically along toward the Gulf of California.

Slocum slapped the ground beside him. Wagner sat. "We're out, we're out!" he cried. "I gotta admit it, you did it, you did it!"

"Kid," Slocum said, "our troubles are just beginnin'."

"You want an adjournment to cooler diggin's," Wagner said. "I'll second it."

Slocum looked at him with a smile. He was beginning to like Wagner's attitude.

8

Slocum said, "Whisper from now on. We need guns. Cartridges. We'll see where we can pick 'em up. We'll just lay low till dark."

He got on his hands and knees and crawled to the eastern end of the marsh. Wagner followed. Stretching eastward was an alkali flat of blinding white. Scattered erratically through it were sand dunes. Some of them were sixty feet high. Much further to the east—Slocum estimated the distance to be about thirty miles—was a harsh, jagged line of mountains. No vegetation, not even sagebrush, was to be seen anywhere.

Not far from the edge of the marsh was a group of adobe houses. Goats browsed on the sparse vegetation which managed to soak up some water from the occasional storms that swirled up from the Gulf of California. Slocum was pleased. Since no one would figure he would head that way, that way was the route he would choose.

•   •   •

"Ain't no water that way," Perkins grumbled.

His dirty forefinger touched the map spread out on Borden's desk.

"You really got fooled, Perkins," Borden said. "It's gonna go bad for you. Unless."

"Unless what?" Perkins's throat was still dry from the gag that Slocum had shoved in it. Borden just looked at him. Perkins seethed in a suppressed rage.

"Unless you ketch 'im."

Perkins sighed. He tapped the double line of the railroad north of Yuma. "I'd ride up this way. Head for the railroad. This upgrade here. He'd ketch a slow freight on the upgrade. Er wait next to this water tank here. They gotta fill the boiler for the long run across the desert."

"Yeah," grunted Borden. "Makes sense. You run over to the marshal's office. Tell 'im I want a posse right away. We'll start in half an hour. You come too. You're gonna enjoy it."

"Damn sure."

"An' if it looks like they're gonna resist arrest—" Borden began.

Perkins lifted a hand and pulled an imaginary trigger.

"I sure ain't gonna be sorry," Borden said with a grin.

Wagner started to crawl to the river's edge. He was going to fill his canteen. The heat was agonizing. His clothes were drenched with sweat.

Don't move.

Slocum's soft, intense voice had steel in it. Wagner recognized it and froze. In his right hand Slocum held a five-foot-long piece of driftwood, thick around as his wrist.

Coiled one foot to the side of Wagner's right hand were

the brown coils of a diamondback. It had slithered to the river for a drink, and was waiting for the sun to go down before it moved back into the desert.

Slocum placed the end of the driftwood right in front of the snake. It struck immediately. He slid the wood under the snake's belly and lifted it in the air. It hung helpless, unable to find solid ground for leverage.

Slocum flipped the snake into the river. It splashed, sank, came up, and started to swim ashore.

"Oh, Christ," Wagner muttered.

"Keep your eyes open," Slocum said in a disgusted tone.

Wagner dipped the canteen into the river and watched it gurgle.

"What now?" he asked in a subdued tone.

"We wait till dark."

The posse—composed of three other guards besides Perkins, a deputy marshal named Hughes, and two cowboys who volunteered out of boredom—jogged north along the western bank of the Colorado River.

The sun was broiling. The cowboys muttered that they should have waited till it cooled off.

"Then they mighta caught the express at the tank," Perkins snapped.

"So what? All Borden's gotta do is telegraph ahead to Ogilby or Acolita. They could surround the damn train with a posse an' pull 'em out."

Perkins silently agreed that this, indeed, would have been the sensible thing to do. No one in his right mind would leave the railroad and strike across the desert. A man would have to be crazy to do that. There were plenty of skeletons to prove that this would be the result if Prendergast and Wagner had chosen that route. But if the sheriff at Ogilby or Acolita in the next county were to find them riding the blinds, he'd just roust them out. He'd have no reason to shoot them while attempting to escape, which was exactly what Perkins intended to do.

He wanted those two men for himself. A little amusement with them first, and then he'd shoot them both in the back. Because that was where a man would shoot fleeing prisoners who refused to halt at the word of command.

And that, of course, was just the way Slocum figured that Borden would be thinking. That was precisely why the safest way to escape would be across the desert, the more desolate the better; and that was the one that lay east of them right now.

As long as they could find water.

"Christ Almighty, I'm burnin' up," Wagner said.

Slocum sighed. He began snapping off several armfuls of reeds, well back from the river. Wagner watched with mild interest.

Slocum said harshly, "Do what I do, God damn it."

Wagner slowly began to collect reeds. Slocum stripped the reeds of their feathery plumes. When that was done, he began to plait them into a mat. Wagner imitated him awkwardly. Slocum next picked up several pieces of driftwood that had lodged along the shore. He stuck them in a circle. Then he laid the crude reed mats across the upright ends of the driftwood.

Now they had a *ramada*.

"Say, that's pretty smart," Wagner said grudgingly.

Slocum said nothing. What would really be smart would be to find clothes and weapons and shoes. Their prison garb would be a dead giveaway; their shoes had been ruined by the immersion in the water, and they needed hats. Without those they would suffer from sunstroke within half an hour.

The sun finally began to slide down toward the horizon. Mosquitoes began to fly out of the stagnant ponds that spotted the marsh. They started to bite in the hot, windless air. Wagner slapped at them irritably.

"What d'ya think they're doin' now?" he asked.

Slocum said, "Checkin' along the railroad, the damn fools."

Wagner bit his lip. "Christ," he said finally in a peevish tone, "Christ, *when's* the sun goin' down?"

Slocum looked at him and decided to say nothing.

"I don't see any goddamn tracks," Perkins said.

It was close to sundown. No one had eaten since noon.

"Mebbe they drowned comin' outa the tunnel," someone said hopefully. "If they didn't come here, they're in the river. Betcha they're in the Gulf by now, and et by sharks, yessir!"

"Oh, shit," Perkins muttered. He was beginning to believe that the man was right. No one ever tried to cross the desert, no matter how desperate they were. It was always the railroad.

"Let's head back," he growled finally. "Borden ain't gonna like this one single bit."

"Don't leave the marsh!" Slocum said sharply.

Wagner half turned. "I gotta do *somethin'*," he said. "The skeeters're drivin' me crazy!" He crawled away. Slocum reflected that for some people the hardest thing to do was wait. He hoped that Wagner would use some common sense. Aside from tying the man hand and foot, he couldn't see what he could do.

Wagner returned in five minutes.

"Come," he said. "Come on!" He sounded excited. He crawled back the way he had come. Slocum followed. At the edge of the marsh Wagner parted the reeds, peered, and said triumphantly, "She's still there!"

Slocum looked. He saw a *ramada* on a slope back of an adobe house. The *ramada* was made of *parilla* leaves. Someone had dragged a flat stone up the chaparral-studded slope. From one of the roof beams there hung a beer keg. Several small holes had been drilled in the bottom. It had just been filled with water from the river. Underneath the improvised shower stood a naked Mexican woman in her thirties. She was soaping her long, shining black hair.

"Look at 'er!" Wagner said. "My oh my, wouldn't you like to straddle that one!"

But what attracted Slocum's attention were the two burros munching hay in a ramshackle corral. Saddles hung over the top rail. The bits and bridles hung from pegs jutting from the adobe wall of the house. People did not steal in this neighborhood.

The owner of all this also owned a little general store, for, as Slocum watched with deep interest, a short, fat brown man walked out of the adobe house with a heavy wooden crate. He set it down, went back in, came out again with a crowbar. He pried up the lid of the crate. The nails screeched as they were drawn out. Wagner paid no attention to any of this; he was staring at the naked girl as she soaped her full, heavy brown breasts.

The Mexican man reached into the crate and pulled out stacks of neatly folded jeans and shirts. Slocum felt pleased. Two men wearing prison attire would have attracted immediate attention. Dressed like everyone else, their chances would improve.

This adobe house had to be some kind of general store. There would likely be other things inside they could use.

The shower water stopped flowing. The girl stepped out into the sun. The heat dried her hair in two minutes. Wagner could not tear his eyes away. She slipped a simple white dress with a square neck over her head. She bent over and fluffed up her hair for faster drying.

The short brown man came to the *ramada*. He stopped behind her and cupped her breasts in his hands. She giggled and held his palms tightly.

"Oh, boy," Wagner muttered. The man put an arm around her waist. Farther up the hill from the *ramada* was a small adobe house. Arms around each other's waists, they walked toward the house.

"Oh, man," Wagner went on. "I'd sure like some of that."

Slocum paid no attention. He had observed that the man lived apart from his store. That was a relief. If he had lived inside, like so many small shopkeepers, a nighttime robbery would be very complicated.

He heard the sound of children's voices beyond the two adobe structures. He tugged at Wagner's elbow.

"Shit, I wanna stay an' watch! She's gonna come out."

Slocum jerked Wagner's shirt impatiently. "Keep your voice *down*," he said between his teeth. "The kids might see us. Back up."

Wagner grudgingly retreated.

By five o'clock that afternoon the posse had returned.

"No sign of 'em?" Borden asked angrily. He rolled a pen back and forth across his desk.

"Nope."

"What d'ya think?"

"They drowned."

"Or they got away. If they git away, what's their next step?"

"The desert."

So it would have to be the Yumas. They would be very interested in the fifty-dollar reward for each man. But, Borden mused, they would not be too aggressive about it. They would try hard enough for the hundred bucks. He sighed. "Hitch the buggy," he told Perkins. "I'm ridin' down to see the ol' chief."

"Gonna git a girl?"

"As long as I'm there."

"You wan' us bring 'em back?" The old chief leaned back against the *ramada* post and crossed his legs tailor-fashion.

"Sure."

"One hunnerd dollars."

"Fifty."

"Two men. One hunnert."

"All right. One hundred. I *want* 'em back. But they won't wanna go back with you, savvy?"

"Me savvy. Me bring," Charlie Bear said.

"If they fight an' your men kill 'em, that's all right."

"Why kill 'um? No kill 'um. Wait till sleep. Then—" The old chief slapped his thigh with such speed that Borden jumped.

Borden said, "You kill 'em, that's good."

The old chief lifted his head and stared at Borden. The white man's meaning was very clear.

"But bring the bodies back. One hundred bucks, O.K."

The chief rolled a cigarette and lit it. He smoked it calmly, looking at the dirt floor. Far out in the desert a coyote yelped suddenly. Borden tried to restrain his impatience. He knew enough about Indian customs not to hurry the chief. He forced himself to be still.

The chief continued to smoke the cigarette till so little of it remained that he pinched it between his thumb and index finger. When it became too hot to hold he pinched out the burning tip. He pulled a small flat tin box from his pocket and opened the butt with his fingernail. He dropped in the few shreds of tobacco and snapped the box shut.

Borden wanted to curse as his impatience mounted. With a great effort he kept his face neutral.

"Kill 'um no good," the chief abruptly remarked.

Borden said, "They bad men. You kill 'em, no more bad."

The chief sighed. When the Yuma killed, long and complex cleansing rituals had to be gone through. One had to be sure that the spirits of the dead would not demand vengeance either by causing sickness to the killer, or to his family, or to his horses.

Like the Pimas farther east, the man who killed had to withdraw from all contact from the tribe and his wife for thirty days. He had to build his own *ramada* and live in it. Food was brought to the *ramada* and left outside. Then the medicine man had to be well paid to oversee the cleansing ceremonies and to make sure that no mistake was made. Any error and the way would be left open for the vengeful ghosts of the dead to wreck havoc not only upon the Yuma killers, but also on the entire tribe.

Of what use would a hundred dollars be then?

But the chief knew that if he were to answer immediately the white man would think he had answered quickly, without thinking.

"Me think."

"Think! What's there to think?" Borden was tired and irritable from his hot, thirsty four-hour drive over rough roads.

"Me think," the chief repeated slowly. "You sleep." He pointed to the pile of rabbit-fur skins in a corner. They made a comfortable bed. "We talk in the mornin'. All ri'?"

"All right," Borden muttered. There was no way to speed up an Indian when he wanted to go slow. Half an hour later, one of the chief's young daughters slid in beside him.

9

The lock was a simple one. The door opened without creaking. Slocum stepped lightly inside. Wagner followed him. The man stumbled against a table and recoiled from Slocum's warning glare. Light from the full moon poured in through the small, dirty window.

Along one shelf jeans and shirts were neatly folded. Another shelf held straw sombreros and cheap boots. Slocum reached for a pair of jeans. He heard a scrabbling sound behind him. He whirled around just as a giant mastiff launched its one hundred and fifty pounds at him.

He just had time to think *watchdog*—then he dropped the jeans, reached out, and caught one of the dog's extended forelegs. He spun around. Using the huge dog's impetus, and pulling the dog with him, he suddenly kneeled. The dog smashed upon its back against the dirt floor, hitting with a heavy thump. It grunted in pain. Before it could get to its legs and resume its silent, murderous attack, Slocum grabbed it by its ears and twisted its head as hard as he could.

The neck snapped.

The dog was almost as big as a St. Bernard. It was one of the breed that the Spaniards had brought with them to Mexico in the early fifteen hundreds. Most of them had died out. Slocum certainly had never expected to see one in Arizona.

He waited to see if the noise had attracted any attention.

"What—" began Wagner.

"*Shhh!*"

Wagner fell silent. After a few seconds Slocum said, "Pick out some clothes that fit. Boots. Socks."

"Yes, but—"

"Don't argue for Christ's sake!"

In a few minutes they were dressed.

"Where's your hat?"

"None of 'em fit."

"So you're not takin' any? Man, take a hat! Even if it's too big. That sun'll kill you."

Wagner put on a hat. It came down past his ears. He looked ridiculous, but Slocum was careful not to laugh. "Stuff a neckerchief in it," Slocum said. He took a machete in its leather scabbard and a small oil stone for sharpening. There were no guns. He took a couple of boxes of matches. No food was on the shelves.

"O.K. Let's go."

"That's the biggest goddamn dog I ever saw in my whole life," Wagner said.

"Where's the canteens?" Slocum demanded, paying no attention to Wagner's babble.

"I did what you said. I filled 'em."

Slocum grunted.

He led the way, slinging one canteen over his shoulder. Wagner followed suit.

"And now let's drink." Wagner started to unscrew his canteen.

"The river," Slocum said. "The canteens are for when there is no river. And drink till you burst. We got a long night and a long day ahead of us."

"We walkin'?"

"You see any horses around, let me know, won't you?" Wagner recognized Slocum's sarcasm. He flushed.

It was five hours later.

"Don't," Slocum said.

Wagner had started to unscrew the canteen. They had walked in a southeasterly direction since eleven the night before. The alkali flat was hard. When Wagner began to complain Slocum said briefly, "Sand's worse." Half an hour later Wagner wanted to rest.

"We'll wait till sunrise. Best to keep movin' while it's cool."

There was no vegetation whatsoever on the desolate flats. Hours later, plodding grimly across the alkali, a faint, pearly grey began to glow on the eastern horizon, which was comprised of a row of jagged peaks.

"How 'bout a drink now?"

"Now we start lookin' for shade."

"Shade? What shade? There ain't nothin' 'cept alkali 'n' rocks!"

The granite spine of the Gila Mountains had begun, after several million years, to crumble. The weathered slabs and boulders had begun to slide down the slopes. Eons ago, when the glacier had reached Illinois, there had been snow on the summits of the Gilas; there had been fierce rain-storms. Water had found cracks, frozen into ice, and the hydraulic pressure of the expansion had cracked the granite wide open. Sudden violent cloudbursts had rolled the giant boulders down along rain-formed valleys and gullies. For twenty miles east of the Gilas stretched the outwash plain. It took the shape of an enormous triangle. Its narrow tip pointed into the mountains.

"I'm gettin' blisters," Wagner complained.

Slocum paid no attention. He had finally found what he was searching for: two big boulders, almost touching at their tops. They widened towards their bottoms. A shaded floor was the result.

"We'll stay here till sunset," he said with satisfaction.

He slid to a sitting position. He pulled the canteen from his shoulder, unscrewed the cap, and filled his mouth with the warm water. He rinsed his mouth, and then slowly drank. He handed the canteen to Wagner.

"Do the same," he said.

"We got another canteen!"

"Do what I say!"

"I don't think they drowned," Borden said.

He looked down at the garden. A thin, consumptive prisoner named Harris was hoeing the weeds in a bored, dispirited manner that contrasted unfavorably with Slocum's expertise. The sloppy work angered Borden so much that he turned his back to the garden.

"Why not?" Perkins asked.

"Maybe Wagner drowned. But not the other man. No. He's out there somewheres. Draggin' Wagner with 'im, I'll bet."

"In the Yuma Desert?"

"Yeah."

"Mr. Borden, ain't no one goes into *that* desert."

"He's got to be there."

"I'm tellin' yuh, *no one* goes there. Not even the god-damn Yumas. No water, no cactus; only sidewinders. But if they're there, the Yumas'll find 'em."

"No, they won't."

"They tol' you no?"

"Yep."

Perkins considered. "Well, shit," he said.

"Christ! Two swallers—that's all I get?"

"If you wanna wait till we run across a *tinaja* in the Gilas, yeah, that's all we get."

A *tinaja* was a depression in the rocks where water collected.

The sun was finally going down.

"If we walk in the dark we're gonna keep fallin' down on account of all them stones."

"That's true. But we're not gonna lose water by sweatin' it out every step. So buckle down your mouth and let's go."

Slocum hoisted his canteen to his shoulder. He looked westwards. Pursuit would come from that direction, if it came at all. It looked as if his ploy for the desert was working. He was surprised that Wagner had not yet complained about being hungry, but that grievance was bound to come.

Borden said, "The son of a bitch said 'Me no go.' Somethin' about their goddamn religion."

"What the hell's their religion got to do with trackin'?"

Borden looked at him without expression.

"Oh," Perkins said, with sudden understanding. "Yeah."

•   •   •

"Jesus! I ain't gonna eat *that!*"

Slocum paid no attention. His swift machete stroke had neatly sliced the head off a sidewinder. It had been wriggling violently as it tried to bury itself under a bed of loose sand.

"Meat," Slocum said shortly. He had noticed mescal growing farther up, on the slope of a small ravine that opened up to their right. Roasted mescal and rattlesnake was filling. He had eaten it before.

With his machete he dug out several mescal roots. Then he dug out a small pit. He regretted dulling the blade, but he would find a stone and strop it sharp again.

"While I'm diggin'," he instructed Wagner, "get some flat stones and a lot of dry brush."

When the pit was dug he laid the stones on the bottom. He placed the dried brush on top of the stones. He set the brush afire and sent Wagner searching for more brush. When the stones were hot enough, he set the mescal roots on top of the stones, the chunks of rattlesnake on top of the roots. He covered everything with dried brush, then brushed the dirt back on top.

"Apache oven," he said to the fascinated Wagner.

"You 'spect *me* to eat *rattlesnake?*"

"Suit yourself. Tastes like chicken. We need meat. Tell you one thing, kid. I'm not gonna carry you if you get too weak to walk."

He sat cross-legged waiting for the food to bake. When it was ready Wagner was famished. He limited himself to mescal.

Perkins walked in without knocking. Borden was staring out the window. As the penitentiary regulations demanded, he had written down the details about the escape. When the report reached the governor, he was sure that there would be an investigation, and someone might turn up his dealings with the merchants in town.

He swung around and demanded, "Ain't you got any manners?"

Perkins smiled with malicious pleasure. "Marshal just come by. Asked did have any room to stick in four 'paches."

"Apaches? What the hell're four Apaches doin' this far west?"

Perkins shrugged. "Dunno. Din't ask. He said jail's full."

The marshal and Borden were old friends.

"How long?" Borden asked, simmering down.

"Two days. They're waitin' fer the next train east to San Carlos."

"They from San Carlos?"

"Yeah."

"Must be Chiricahuas."

"Mebbe."

"How come they're this far west?"

Perkins shrugged.

Borden asked, "They got passes?"

A sudden idea had burst upon him. The Chiricahuas were hard people and skilled desert trackers. They had no weird religious beliefs which made murder complicated. As for passes, the Indian agent at each reservation could issue passes permitting the bearer to leave the reservation, usually to go hunting. If they didn't have the pass in their possession, they could be picked up as renegades.

"Yeah, they got passes. Look, why don't you talk to the marshal? He's drinkin' a cup a coffee down in the kitchen right now."

Borden shoved his chair back. He walked downstairs, along a stone corridor, and into the penitentiary kitchen.

Gilroy, the marshal, was eating a doughnut and drinking black coffee from a chipped white mug.

"All right with you, Borden?" he asked.

"Sure. You got their passes?"

Gilroy nodded. He was busy chewing. He reached into a shirt pocket and hauled out the four stained and dirty passes.

"Can I keep 'em?"

"Sure. Give 'em back when you set 'em on the train."

Borden watched the marshal wipe his lips with his sleeve. He felt excited. He got up, nodded abstractedly as Gilroy left. He walked to the holding cell. The four Apaches from San Carlos were sitting cross-legged on the floor.

The biggest one demanded cigarettes.

They wore filthy white cotton shirts which hung outside their dirty, unwashed pants. The pants were stuck inside their knee-high buckskin moccasins. All four wore red cotton headbands to keep their shoulder-length black hair in place. Their jet-black eyes stared at him impassively.

"You White Mountain or Chiricahua?" Borden asked.

They were silent.

"You gimme passes," the big one demanded harshly. He was clearly their leader, Borden saw. Without passes they would be harassed and thrown into jails all across the territory.

Borden tossed in cigarette papers and a sack of Bull Durham. He pulled out a small box of friction matches and tossed it in.

When they were puffing away contentedly the leader suddenly said, "Chiricahua."

Borden smiled. Better and better. The Chiricahuas, unlike the White Mountains or the Mescaleros, were experienced desert travelers.

"What's your name?"

"Alchisay. What you?"

"Well, Alchisay, first thing you gotta understand, you gotta have manners." He moved closer to the bars so that no one except the Apaches could listen. "Let's cut a deal."

"Manners?" Alchisay was puzzled at the word.

"You don't ask me my name," Borden said. "I tell you when I *feel* like it, see?" He felt that the situation was getting away from him, and he wisely decided to yield. "My name is Superintendent Borden."

He could see that Alchisay thought that "Superintendent" was his first name. While Alchisay mouthed the word, trying it out for correct pronunciation, Borden went on, still in the same low tone, "You do what I say. You'll get your passes back, an' fifty dollars silver for each man, and then a free ride on the train to San Carlos."

"'baccy?"

"An' all the tobacco you want, yes."

Alchisay grinned. "O.K. You gimme money."

"First," Borden said, "first, you bring me back two heads."

But the problem for the four Apaches was where to pick up the trail.

Here is where luck entered. Belisario Robles, who owned the little general store that Slocum had robbed, was busily complaining about the theft to Guillermo Gonzalez in the dilapidated tin-roofed shack that served as a cantina for the Mexicans who lived on the east side of the Colorado River.

This caused a great deal of hilarity, since Robles was regarded as a thief himself because of the excessive prices he charged for substandard products. No one was sorry about the dead dog, which was a surly brute that had always growled at everyone.

One man in the appreciative audience was Demetrio Gomez. He was describing the conversation to Frank Reed, one of the prison guards. Reed knew Robles. He mentioned the theft idly to Perkins as they were eating supper.

Perkins quietly got up and knocked on the door to Borden's apartment. Mrs. Borden opened the door. It was the usual hot, sticky Yuma evening, and all she was wearing was a thin blue cotton robe.

"Well?" she said coldly. She didn't like Perkins and she made no bones about her dislike.

"Mr. Borden."

She turned without a word. Perkins whistled tunelessly while he waited. He envied Slocum, who had gotten closer to that ripe ass that he ever would. But the information he was about to hand to Borden might make amends.

"Yeah, Perkins?"

"I think we got 'em."

"What?"

"Someone bust into Belisario Robles's place across the river last night."

"Hurry up, I'm eatin' supper!"

"An' took two pairs of pants, two pairs of boots. Two shirts. Two hats. A machete. What's that sound like?"

Borden said with a grin, "Gonna unleash them Cherrycahuas; good place to start 'em. Thanks."

The Chiricahuas paced around Robles's store. The ground was baked hard by the sun and, of course, they found nothing. Borden watched with a frown. Alchisay headed for the riverside, where Slocum and Wagner had waited till dark. Alchisay beckoned him over. The Apaches pointed at the flattened reeds where the two men had waited.

"Yeah," he said, grinning. "Yep! They been here."

He turned and looked at the four Chiricahuas. They wore knives at their belts. Each man carried a pouch stuffed with jerky. Borden had handed each one a canteen.

"How come you know they holed up here?" Borden asked out of curiosity.

"Me wanna hide, me hide there."

"Where you think they went?"

Alchisay lifted his chin towards the distant hills across the alkali flats.

"I ain't so sure," Borden said skeptically. "No water."

"'paches find water. Mebbe so them fellers find water."

"Easy enough to check out," Perkins said. "Jesus, look at 'em! Like huntin' dogs on a leash!"

"See if you c'n cut their trail," Borden said. He felt a thrill as he thought of what they would do to Prendergast and Wagner when they caught them. Apaches were very inventive when it came to torture.

The four Chiricahuas moved past him at a ground-eating jog-trot. Borden watched as they moved past the adobe houses, heading east toward the desert.

The Mexicans stared at them. Apaches and Mexicans hated each other and had done so for centuries. But the presence of the two officials reduced the tension. Suddenly Alchisay let out a sharp whistle. When Borden panted his way up, Alchisay pointed to the ground.

In the alkali crust there were two sets of bootprints, heading east.

"New boots," Alchisay said. He indicated the outlines of the prints. "New. Even, all 'roun'."

Borden remembered that Robles had complained that the thief had stolen two pairs of boots.

"How long ago?"

Alchisay grunted an order. The short, heavily muscled

Apache named Ditoh kneeled. He brought his face close to
the prints, then wet a finger and held it up. A slight breeze
had been blowing from the north since sunrise. He spoke
in guttural Apache. Alchisay looked at the bottoms of the
prints. The wind had blown grains of sand into the heel
portions. He grunted approval.

"He say las' night."

Borden turned to Perkins. "What d'ya think?" he asked.

"I bet it's them."

Alchisay said, with a thin smile, "We ketchum. You bet."

Ditoh grinned. If the white man only wanted the heads,
he and the other Chiricahuas knew how to amuse themselves
for a few hours before they would separate the heads from
what remained of the torsos.

10

The mescal wasn't so bad, Wagner decided. He chewed the pulp and spat out the stringy fibers that remained. He refused, however, to eat the chunks of rattlesnake. Slocum calmly chewed away; he was amused by Wagner's look of nausea.

"I ain't never gonna eat snake," Wagner said.

"You will when you're hungry."

"I ain't *that* hungry yet."

Slocum sipped from the canteen and sloshed the remainder around. There were two long swallows left. With luck they might reach a *tinaja* by mid-morning of the next day; such tiny lakes of rainwater might be found anywhere in the rocky spines of the Gila Mountains.

The terrain was too rocky to negotiate at night. They would have to set off as soon as there was enough light. Slocum kicked the hot stones from the mescal pit. Lined up in a row, they provided a sort of radiator which gave off heat for several hours. Wagner fell asleep first. He slept in a curled-up position, with his hands pressed between his thighs. He snored loudly, a dangerous habit in Indian territory. Slocum woke him up and told him to quit snoring.

"How the hell c'n I?" demanded the sleepy Wagner.

"You better," Slocum said. "Because I'm gonna keep wakin' you up till you sleep with your mouth closed."

"Aw, shit," Wagner muttered, and fell asleep instantly. Slocum woke him up twice more in the next hour, to the accompaniment of Wagner's angry curses. But after the third time, even in his sleep, Wagner kept his mouth closed.

The stones felt good against Slocum's back. If luck would be with them, two days' hard travelling should put them across the border into Mexico. And three more days should put them into Puerto Peñasco, where Mr. Wagner should be waiting with his twenty-nine thousand, five hundred. And only two days over the one-month time limit. He fell asleep.

Alchisay held up his hand. The other three Apaches stopped. Alchisay took a long inhalation. He grunted in satisfaction. The others, less sensitive, then caught the aroma of roasted mescal. They stared at one another. Only Apaches roasted mescal; but this was not Apache territory.

Alchisay chewed his lip and thought hard. The tracks they were following led up the slope from where the smell of the mescal was coming. Alchisay finally said, "The People are here."

Ditoh said immediately, "But the Belighanna—"

"Belighanna" was the Apache corruption of "American."

"The People saw them coming. They killed them. Now they are eating."

The others nodded. If the People were there, they would know from their scouts that the clumsy Belighanna would walk right into their ambush.

Alchisay said with a smile, "They will not begrudge us two heads."

Ditoh grunted his assent. The other two men, Delchay and Nantije, lacked initiative; they always agreed with Ditoh and Alchisay. The four men next moved up the slope. They made no attempt to move silently. It was good manners never to approach any Apache camp quietly. Enemies did that. So the men talked loudly in the Chiricahua dialect.

Slocum woke instantly. Wagner was sleeping with his mouth closed and making no snoring sound. He placed a hand over Wagner's mouth. As the startled man awoke, he whispered, "Someone comin'. *Don't talk*. Follow me."

He stood up and slung the canteen over his shoulder. He picked up the machete and moved diagonally up the slope. There was a dense matting of scrub oak growing because of the higher rainfall. Once inside the area, he suddenly heard the sounds of Chiricahua Apache.

"God damn it," he whispered.

"What?"

"Take your boots off," he said quietly.

"What—" Wagner began.

"Godalmighty," he hissed in a fury, "take 'em off, you asshole!"

Wagner pulled them off in a sullen manner. He did not know that any Apache, with a torch made from dried *sacatón,* could follow their boot tracks. But following a track made with bare feet was so faint that the pursuit would have to wait for morning and better light.

The pebbles were sharp. Wagner had suddenly heard the guttural Apache conversation; he had sense enough to keep silent, even though cactus thorns and dried twigs with spiky little branches littered the hard, stony soil.

As the two men made their way slowly and painfully, Slocum turned and looked downward towards their camp. Ditoh had made a torch and was beginning to follow their trail.

Wagner whispered, "They followin' us? *Shit*." Slocum didn't care for it either, but there was one consolation: Wagner did not have to be prodded to be quiet or to make time.

Ditoh looked at the boot tracks. He looked up with a puzzled expression.

Alchisay said, "The Belighanna cooked the mescal. Like the People. And they have left; they heard us making too much noise." He stared into the darkness. It was too risky to follow.

"We will catch up with them in the morning. In the meantime, they left us some warm stones." He felt pleased. For a moment, when he thought that the People had been torturing the two Belighanna, he had felt disappointed. Now, since the Belighanna were in good health, he would have the pleasure of exercising his imagination when he caught them.

So that amusement was to come some time next morning.

"We are tired. Let us sleep. Ditoh, first watch."

Slocum looked down the slope at the Apaches' small fire. Wagner sat cross-legged opposite him and worked out a cactus thorn from his heel. He cursed steadily in a monotone.

"How long we gonna walk barefoot?"

Slocum thought that if they went barefoot any longer,

their feet would become so crippled that they wouldn't be able to walk at all. Their best bet lay in making good time. That would leave a very obvious trail—but there was no other way out of their dilemma. Sooner or later, luck would come along. He hoped it would be good luck.

"Put 'em on."

"Muchas gracias."

Slocum didn't care for the sarcasm. But by now most of Wagner's ill-tempered remarks were like mosquitoes. If they came too closely together they would be infuriating, but an occasional one could be swatted aside.

There was more vegetation. The moisture-filled winds from the Gulf of California dropped their load of rain as the mountains forced them upwards. *Ocotillo* was frequent. From time to time they would brush against a jumping *cholla* and Wagner started a low, monotonous cursing as the hooked spines fell on their hands and dug into their skin. He stopped to pull them out.

Slocum shoved him. "Keep *goin'*," he said between his teeth. "Play doctor tomorrow. They're gonna pick up our trail soon's the sun comes up. An' we don't have anything to fight with 'cept one machete. So, keep a-goin'."

Wagner was scared enough to mute his vituperation. They moved on, slipping on slick rocks and stumbling against bunches of low, coarse *sacatón*. The moon rose after 2:00 A.M. Its full pour of light enabled them to make much better time. Slocum kept turning around to watch their back trail. Wagner, in much worse physical condition, kept panting as they moved along one of the southward-trending ridges.

Ditoh said, "The Belighanna put their boots on here."

Nantije, the smallest and youngest, laughed. "Their feet

hurt too much," he said. The Apaches' own feet were so calloused from childhood on that, if necessary, they could walk without moccasins.

They continued their effortless, gliding walk. Within three hours, Alchisay guessed, they would come up with the two Belighanna. Then the fun would begin. Afterwards, he would dump the two heads in the old flour sack he had had the foresight to take along. Then they would head back to Yuma and the one hundred dollars reward.

Seldom had he had been able to combine pleasure with profit.

Slocum stopped short. They had come to a depression in the rocky surface. Something was shining at the bottom. It was round, made of steel, and there was a ridge along the top. He bent down and picked it up. A human skull rolled out. Wagner jumped.

Slocum held the steel object up to the moonlight. It was an old Spanish helmet of the sixteenth century. When he looked down he could see the rest of the skeleton. It shone inside the steel cuirass worn by a foot soldier. A rusted object nearby turned out to be a crossbow. The leather boots had rotted away, but the rusty, cruel Spanish spurs lay beside the ankle bones.

"What the hell's that?" Wagner demanded.

"Other people had trouble around here," Slocum said dryly. Just about where the throat would be—but it had been torn out by some wild animal—lay a stone head of an arrow. The wooden shaft had long ago rotted away.

"Let's get away from here," Wagner said. "It gives me the willies."

The sky was greying quickly in the east. The bottom, close to the horizon, was flushing pink. He saw a thin stream of smoke rising straight up in the windless air.

In this country that demanded investigation.

"Stay here," Slocum said briefly. He didn't want Wagner doing something wrong from which it would take trouble to extricate him. He took off his straw sombrero, grabbed a bunch of bear grass, and tied it around his head with a long stalk. He edged up to the crest of the ridge and looked down. He saw a valley one mile long and three hundred yards wide. Grass grew stirrup-high. He counted a hundred and thirty-four head of cattle grazing contentedly along the length of the valley. There were thirteen head of three-year-olds ready to ship.

The smoke emerged from the chimney of an adobe house built on the slope nearest him. A well-built, sturdy corral framed the house on its north side. A chicken coop was on the west side. Someone had made himself a small paradise here.

As Slocum watched, a woman stepped out of the house. She stood in the doorway for a moment holding a small Navajo rug. She flapped it so sharply that Slocum could hear the slapping reports. He smiled. To see these familiar sights, which belonged somewhere in the placid, settled East instead of on this violent, dangerous frontier, made him shake his head in amazement. The woman wore a short-sleeved grey dress. The air was still chilly, and she wrapped her arms around her body and shivered. Her long yellow hair hung down her back. She was a trifle plump, but Slocum found her attractive. She turned her face to the sun and with her eyes closed, she began to comb her hair.

Slocum's mother used to do that on their farm in Georgia. He watched with longing. All that was done with; the War had ruined everything. She had died in the last winter of the war of pneumonia, after the Yankees had burned her house and there was no more firewood anywhere within miles. Slocum tore his mind away from the past.

He watched as she walked briskly to the chicken coop, found five eggs under the setting hens, turned around, and went back into the house. He thought it was a dangerous place to live in, even with a man. The fact that this range was on no major route might have made it less tempting to bandits or renegade Apaches.

Then he smelled bacon frying. Saliva poured into his mouth. It looked safe. He turned and slid down.

"What's up?" Wagner asked sleepily.

"Stay here. I'm goin' down for a look."

"O.K. Sure." Wagner didn't care as long as he could go on sleeping.

Slocum went up to the ridgetop again. At the crest he turned and looked at their back trail. He saw nothing. It seemed likely that the Indians they had seen last night had lost interest in them. And if Wagner was asleep, at least he would stay out of trouble.

Slocum moved carefully down the slope toward the adobe house. He had never expected to see anyone living in such a harsh wilderness, but there were people who liked privacy and were willing to accept the risk that entailed.

This also meant being ready to fight at any time.

He began whistling loudly when he got within two hundred yards. When he had cut that distance in half he began yelling, "Hello, the house!" And, in case they were Mexicans— there were Spaniards who had blonde hair—he added, *"Buenos dias!"*

Alchisay looked down at the stupid Belighanna. The man was asleep—in broad daylight! It had been childishly easy to surround him while he was snoring, seize him, and tie him hand and foot with rawhide thongs.

Wagner lay terrified. Alchisay was convinced that the other Belighanna had left this one behind, probably because he was so obviously stupid and incompetent.

Delchay and Nantije stripped Wagner naked. Alchisay decided to amuse himself with this one for half an hour or so. Then he would take the head and catch up with the other one. No Belighanna that Alchisay had ever met could cover as much ground as an Apache. They would probably catch up about sunset, and he would get the same treatment. Twenty-four hours later, Alchisay would empty the flour sack on the white chief's desk, collect the money and their passes, and go back to San Carlos with some good stories to boast about at the campfires.

There was a piñon nearby. To a horizontal branch they attached the stupid one's ankles so that the top of his head hung ten inches above the ground.

Alchisay said briefly, "Make a fire."

Ditoh grinned and started to collect firewood.

Slocum halted fifty feet from the front door and waited patiently. He was not at all surprised when she suddenly stepped out the door with a heavy Springfield rifle. She held it, Slocum noticed, with the kind of cool competence that meant that she knew how to use it. It was a powerful and accurate weapon, and Slocum intended to give it plenty of respectful attention.

"Turn around real slow, mister," she said.

He complied. It was clear that she wanted to check him for any concealed weapon. Satisfied at last, she nodded. "You c'n come closer. Where's your hoss?"

No one travelled without a horse.

"Pulled up the picket pin 'n' run away," he told her.

"I suspect y' had a Colt. Where's it?"

"Had it hung over the horn." It was an unlikely place for it, but she did not suspect any lie. Satisfied, she lowered the Springfield.

"'Spect you're hongry?"

"Yes'm."

"Come in an' set." She turned. Obviously, she was completely assured of his being harmless.

The interior of the place was spotless. The floor was made of mud that had been smoothed with a trowel and then hardened with animal blood. A man's worn clothes hung on pegs set in the adobe wall. Her single spare dress and a sunbonnet hung on similar pegs.

She noticed Slocum's glance at the clothes. "My man. He's in the mine," she said.

"A mine? *Here?*"

"He found some color up there, t'other side o' the ridge. Two years ago it were. Came back 'n' built this house fer me. Then we got married."

Slocum wolfed down the bacon and eggs she had prepared. When he had satisfied his hunger, he asked, "Pretty risky, isn't it?"

"I c'n shoot good, stranger. I ain't worried none. Been shootin' since I was eight. Sorry 'bout your hoss. We ain't got but one, 'n' Pete's got it over to th' mine. An' this ain't country fer a man without a gun. We got an extry gun. S'pose you could have it. Where you headin'?"

"Up towards the Gila," Slocum said immediately. He was going in the opposite direction, but she would know that he was fleeing from the law if she knew he was going toward Mexico. And then she might not lend him the gun, because Slocum felt that she was going to ask him to drop it off somewhere where her Pete could pick it up some day.

"A fur piece."

"You from Georgia?" he asked abruptly.

"I am, mister."

Slocum grinned. "Me, too."

A big smile spread over her face. She poked around in an old wooden crate in a corner and found a box of cartridges. Next she reached under the bed and pulled out a long object wrapped in an old grey blanket that had seen better days.

She unwrapped the blanket. Inside was a Winchester carbine.

"Pete bought it when we fust came. But it ain't no good fer deer. A Springfield carries way further. You c'n borry it. Just drop it off at Wellton on yer way to the Gila. Leave it at Jenkins's place. Can't miss it nohow."

"Much obliged, and thank you kindly," Slocum said. Sooner or later he would pass by Wellton.

"Your hoss prob'ly will wind up here. Pete'll take it with 'im next time he goes to Wellton. He'll leave it at Jenkins's place."

"Much obliged." He was jubilant. The vague tension of being stuck in the Yuma Desert with only a machete fell away. He sighted up the barrel. It was clean; there was no dust, lint, or powder.

"I'll just mosey along, then, ma'am," he said. "Gonna track my horse. I hope the son of—excuse me, ma'am—I hope he went and caught the reins in some chaparral."

"How 'bout some water?"

"Got plenty in my canteen." He slapped it.

She had run out of small talk. He was the first person besides her husband she had seen for five months. It was with wistful reluctance that she watched him stride away.

Just before he reached the ridge he dropped down, even

though he was sure that all he would see would be the
snoring Wagner. He never took anything for granted. That
was how he had managed to survive all his years in the
West. People who took things for granted ended up in a
cemetery, if they were lucky, or their bones rotted away in
some obscure arroyo where they had been ambushed. He
crawled up to a clump of densely matted mesquite that was
growing along the crest. He took off his sombrero and
peered down.

Wagner's hair was on fire. He was screaming in agony.

Slocum picked out the Apache who seemed to be in
charge. It was Alchisay, who was standing back with his
arms folded. Slocum lay flat. He began his calculations to
allow for the drop in the bullet's flight. But at that moment
Ditoh reached out and grabbed Wagner's penis in his left
hand. His right hand held a knife.

There was no time left for careful aiming. Slocum swung
the barrel at Ditoh and fired a snap shot. The bullet was
too high and too far to the right. It seared Ditoh's left cheek
instead of hitting him dead center in the chest.

At the sound of the Winchester's crack, the four Apaches
instantly reacted. They went flat into the chaparral, rolled
over, and sprinted for the shelter of a wild jumble of boulders. They ran at a crouch, weaving and ducking. Slocum
fired twice, but all he managed to do was to send up two
little spurts of dust a few feet to their right.

"Shit," Slocum said. He stopped firing. There was no
point in wasting cartridges until he had sighted in the carbine.

As he figured, there was no sign of them once he had
rounded the boulder area. First things first; Wagner could
wait. His hair was all right. Slocum had kicked out the fire
as he ran by.

They had climbed the ridge to the west and were lost somewhere in dense chaparral. He was not going to follow four Apaches in ideal ambush country. He turned around and walked back. Wagner was still hanging, head down. His hair had burned off and the red skin underneath was beginning to blister.

"Where the fuck were you?" he yelled, his face contorted in rage.

Slocum said, "Shut up," and found the machete, which the Apaches had not found. With his left arm he held Wagner by his thighs while he slashed the rawhide that lashed his ankles to the piñon branch. Slocum eased him to the ground and cut his wrist bonds.

"Jesus, it hurts," Wagner moaned. He put his palms on top of his head and flinched as he felt the blisters. "Look what the red bastards did!"

"Shouldn't wonder it hurts," Slocum said. "Get dressed. You oughta to be glad they couldn't finish. Not many escape from an Apache torture session."

Wagner picked up his pants. "They grabbed me an' before I knew it, I was hoisted. Then they lit this goddamn fire, and then one of 'em grabbed my—"

Slocum let him talk it out. When Wagner had run down, he said gently, "Put your boots on. We're movin' on."

For once Wagner heartily agreed. Only when they had been walking for half an hour did it suddenly dawn on him that Slocum was carrying a Winchester.

"Jesus, where did *that* come from?"

"A lady loaned it to me."

It was typical of the man's lack of fitness for the frontier that it had taken him this long to make the observation. Of course, Slocum mused, if it had been brought to his attention, he would have yelled that there were other things on his mind. And Slocum, if this conversation had actually occurred, would have said mildly that it was the men who observed—even in agony—who were the survivors.

But he kept silent.

"A *lady?* Bullshit!"

"Just keep movin', Russell."

"You gonna tell me where you got it?"

Slocum suddenly lost his temper. "No," he said between gritted teeth, "I'm *not* gonna tell you where I got it."

Wagner looked at his face and dropped the subject. "I bet they're layin' up somewhere waitin' for us," he said nervously.

"Nope. Not when we got a gun. It's too risky for 'em. They don't take chances. They play the odds, but only when it's in their favor. They'll go off now and look for an easy mark. Move!"

Slocum was worried, but he didn't want Wagner to know. A man in charge who lets his worry be sensed has set his command on the road to despair and defeat. The moccasin patterns left in the dust showed that they were Chiricahuas. He had no idea why they were here, so far from their traditional range, over three hundred miles to the east. There were two deserts and two enemy tribes—the Pimas and the Papagoes—in between.

Whatever the reason, they had better put distance between themselves and the four Chiricahuas. One man who was competent—himself—and one who would have to be nursed every foot of the way were an easily gobbled snack for these Apache wolves.

"My head hurts," came a familiar whine.

"I believe you. *Move*, damn it!"

And wolves never gave up easily.

• • •

Alchisay had seen the smoke rising on the far side of the ridge. Now that the hard Belighanna had stopped trailing them, it would be a good idea to take a look at the smoke. It might turn out to be profitable.

They trotted north along the base of the ridge. They were in superb physical condition. From childhood on, Apaches were trained to endurance. By the time an Apache boy was fifteen he could usually beat the average cavalry soldier in physical combat.

They angled up toward the crest. Just below the crest they halted. No words were necessary. They behaved like the traditional war party; no one challenged Alchisay's decisions, since it was obvious that he was usually right.

It had been his idea to get the passes from the agent at San Carlos. He had actually wept real tears when he told the agent, a naive, well-meaning Quaker named Atkins, that his children were starving and needed deer meat. If he and three friends were to get the passes, they would hunt up on the Natanes Plateau. There they would dry the meat into jerky and then return. Atkins consulted with knowledgeable people about the Natanes. He found out that there were no ranchers in the area. That meant to him that the possibility of an Apache–white clash did not exist. Therefore, he granted the request.

The agent was a fool. None of the four men had a woman or any children. As soon as they had the passes in their hands they headed southwest for the Gila road. There they killed four travellers in seven days. They carefully buried the watches and the money they found. They planned to dig up the buried loot on their triumphant return journey. They would sell the watches to the post trader at Fort Thomas; the man could be relied upon to keep his mouth shut. With the money they would buy deer jerky from the Pimas and go back. The agent would see the jerky and would be happy that his charges showed peaceful instincts for a change. Then they would boast of their adventures and laugh at the stupidity of the agent.

Alchisay tore off some tufts of *sacatón*. He tied it around his head and slowly lifted his head over the crest.

He saw the house and an empty corral. Good. That meant the man was not there. He saw washing flapping on a line. That meant there was a woman.

He gave instructions to Ditoh. These lonely places usually produced women who knew how to shoot. A man had to be careful. Ditoh went down first. He made a wide circle through the chaparral, and then, lower down, through the grassy valley. Finally, when he was ready, he dropped to his hands and knees and approached the front door as if he were sick and not strong enough to walk.

That was sure to attract her total attention. Alchisay had thought up the trick years before, and it always worked. People thought that a wounded or sick man could not be a threat, so her guard would be down.

Alchisay moved like a windblown seed till he stood around a corner of the house from the front door. Ditoh lifted his head and looked at Alchisay for instructions. Alchisay nodded and drew his knife.

Ditoh let out a long, agonized moan. Something stirred within the house. Then a woman suddenly appeared in the doorway, holding a Springfield rifle. She seemed scared. Alchisay grinned. He had always wanted a Springfield. Eskiminzin, the chief, had one. Whenever Alchisay paid him for the cartridges—and Eskiminzin charged plenty!—the chief let him fire it. So he knew how to fire one.

As soon as Ditoh saw the woman he let out an even more agonized groan. She started to walk toward him. Alchisay stepped behind her in three long, silent strides.

She heard him at the last second. Her terrified face turned toward him. His left forearm went around her neck. His right hand shoved his knife into her right kidney up to the hilt.

She dropped the rifle and brought both hands in back of her. Both hands clawed at Alchisay's thighs. He pulled the knife out and rammed it in again. She let out a choked scream and sagged. He let her drop. She would be dead within five minutes, Alchisay estimated.

Ditoh got to his feet. He passed her with a casual glance and walked into the house. Delchay joined him. While the two others searched for food, Alchisay sought Springfield ammunition. He found two boxes of it in a wooden crate in a corner of the room.

He grunted with pleasure. Now he could go after the two Belighanna on an equal footing. On a shelf next to the fireplace he found a clay jug full of molasses. He drank half of it and passed the jug to Ditoh. Ditoh refused it; he preferred to munch away at the raw onions he found hung across a wooden peg. There was a haunch of venison hanging from a hook next to the simple fireplace.

They cut steaks and broiled them, then squatted and ate.

Alchisay said that the woman's husband had gone away on his horse. They should look for him and, after killing him, they could cut his horse's throat and eat it. Apaches liked horse meat, which they considered superior to beef or even venison. After that business was taken care of, Alchisay added, they could then proceed to the real business of the expedition and track the two Belighanna.

Alchisay was nervous about the dead woman. He feared vengeance from her spirit, which was right this second hanging around the house. Indeed, whenever an Apache died, the *jacal* where the death occurred was immediately burned. Then the whole camp moved on and felt better, since the ghost would be tied to the place where the death had taken place. There the malevolent spirit would hover in rage. But it would be harmless as long as no one came into the area.

So the men were happy to leave.

Six miles away the horse tracks ended in an arroyo. There they came upon the horse eating clumps of sparse grass. It had been hobbled. The horse looked up with mild interest at the Apaches. Then it went back to its grazing. The Apaches moved warily up the chaparral-studded slope till they saw the mine opening. From inside came the faint clanging sound of a six-pound jack smacking a chisel.

Alchisay prodded Ditoh with the muzzle of the Springfield. Ditoh released an annoyed grunt. Alchisay had decided to try the same trick that had worked so well with the miner's woman. He believed that if something worked well he should do it again.

Ditoh climbed the rocks that formed the mine dump. He waited till Alchisay and Nantije had taken their positions on either side of the mine opening. Satisfied, Alchisay took out his knife and waited. He was not going to fire a single Springfield cartridge till he absolutely had to. They were too hard to get, and he still remembered how much Eski-minzin had charged him for each one.

Ditoh lay flat on the rocks of the mine dump. Alchisay nodded. Ditoh let out a howl of agony. The sledge-hammer noise stopped. Alchisay nodded again and Ditoh howled once more.

The miner appeared at the mine opening. He held a Colt in his right hand. A full cartridge belt was buckled around his waist. Alchisay's eyes sparkled. A Springfield was fine, but a Colt, too! With a full cartridge belt!

The miner took a wary step toward the prostrate Ditoh. Alchisay took a long step toward the man's back. A small rock he stepped on was badly balanced. Alchisay lost his equilibrium and fell full length.

The miner whirled. He fired just as Alchisay gained his feet and lunged at him. The slug blasted Alchisay's little finger on his right hand and left a splinter of bone showing. The finger was splattered against the rock. A fraction of a second later, Alchisay's knife had gone up to the hilt in the man's stomach. He sank to his knees. He gripped the knife hilt—with Alchisay's hand still holding it—and the two men wrestled in grim silence for the knife. Ditoh came up from behind, pulled the man's head back by the hair, and cut his throat with a savage left-to-right slash. Bright arterial blood gushed over Alchisay's hands and chest. When he was dead, Alchisay unbuckled the man's gunbelt and put it on. He pulled the Colt from the miner's dead hand. He ripped the grey shirt and used it as a rag to wipe the blood off the gun and his hands.

For a moment he thought that Ditoh would claim the gun for himself, and he was prepared for an argument. But Ditoh said nothing. Nantije suddenly held up Alchisay's shattered finger. Alchisay took it with a relieved grunt. It could be used as a charm if a sorcerer found it. Alchisay turned and walked into the chaparral alone. The others knew what he was going to do, and they waited in respectful silence.

He found a flat rock and turned it over. Ants ran in every direction through their tunnels. Alchisay dug a hole with the point of his knife, placed the finger inside the hole, covered it with his foot, turned the rock again, and walked away. He was sure that no one would ever find it, even an evil sorcerer. His hand began to throb.

He found a beavertail cactus. He broke off a pad, and scraped the needles off with his knife blade. Then he cut away the skin and folded the pad over the stump of his finger. The juice was astringent and helped stop the bleeding.

He rode the horse back to the house while the others walked. He had thought of a use for the woman's clothes he had seen hanging on pegs. The *zapilotes* flapped away at their approach. The eyes were already gone. Later, the coyotes would finish the job.

He sat the horse while Delchay brought out her dress and sunbonnet. It would be too risky for him to go in the house; her spirit would be more likely to be inside the house than outside. Delchay didn't want to go in, but Alchisay forced him. Ditoh sulked; Alchisay knew it was because he wanted the Colt. If her spirit saw Alchisay it might make him sick; it might even make the Springfield misfire.

They killed the horse and ate steaks cut from its hindquarters. Alchisay made Ditoh cut out and clean the intestines. They would come in handy if they were forced to do any desert tracking.

As Alchisay ate, he reconsidered. It had been a profitable little visit. At the cost of a little finger, he now owned a Colt and a Springfield. They had killed two whites. He would have liked to have made the second one's death a long, drawn-out affair, but luck was against him on that score. Still, there were two more to work on when he caught up.

And, what was very important, his status was now high with the others. It would grow with the retelling when they arrived back at San Carlos. The next time he would announce a war party, he could take his pick of applicants. Ditoh was stupid; Nantije was even worse. He could do better.

Now, with his superior firepower, it was time to get down to business.

He estimated that he would catch up with the two men some time the next afternoon. They would have to be careful. The taller of the two looked like he knew his way about. He had baked mescal, Apache style, where another white man would have starved, and he was smart enough to fire at the Apaches from ambush.

But he had missed. So that meant, Alchisay reasoned, as his stump began throbbing, that the tall man was a poor shot.

Still, it would be wise not to underestimate him. Alchisay was sure that the man would never fall for the old trick he had used twice this afternoon. That was why he was taking the woman's clothes along. He had something new in mind.

When Nantije said plaintively, "Why do I have to carry this?" Alchisay said patiently, "Wait. *Wait.*"

11

"Christ, why're you pushin' so hard?"

"There's four of them, an' only two of us. Keep *movin'*."

"Wait. Wait a second, will yuh?"

Wagner unslung his canteen.

"Go easy on that water!" Slocum ordered.

"You said there'd be water up here," Wagner said accusingly.

"Stop bellyachin'. There usually is."

"Jesus, I'm thirsty!"

"So am I, kid. Go easy on that water."

Wagner tilted the canteen, but mindful of Slocum's low, hard-voiced warning, he took only one small swallow. He screwed the cap back on and then shook it defiantly in Slocum's face.

Slocum heard the remaining cupful of water slosh around in it.

"You hear that?" Wagner demanded in a plaintive tone.

Oh, shit, Slocum thought wearily. *I'm stuck with a goddamn baby.* Counting only the time since he had entered Yuma Penitentiary, there were only eight more days to go before the three months would be up. The three months he had promised old man Wagner it would take to spring his son and meet him at the Posada Carapán in Puerto Peñasco.

The thought made him feel better. Hell, he could stand any snot-nosed kid for eight days! And thirty thousand bucks would be waiting for him.

"Move along there, sonny," he said cheerfully. He paid no attention to Wagner's irritated scowl.

There had been a succession of dry years. Rain had been scarce. The few *tinajas* they had come across were dried up. Water had become a serious problem.

Slocum decided to drop down to a lower level. Perhaps he would reach the desert floor; he knew how to extract water from desert plants. He had learned the trick from some Apaches he had once lived with, years ago. So they angled out and down from the groves of scrub oak. Far down one of the narrow *arroyos* which dropped down toward the desert, he had noticed some barrel cactus backed up against a vertical rock face made of lava. Ages ago there had been intense volcanic activity here.

"What're we headin' down for?" demanded Wagner. "At least it's cooler up here, ain't it?" He looked at Slocum as if he were out of his mind.

"See that cactus? We'll get us some water."

Like people who did not know how to live off the desert, Wagner assumed that there would be water inside, as if, indeed, it was a real barrel just filled with water. He brightened.

When they reached it, Slocum set his empty canteen upright on the hard, packed soil. He wedged it tightly into place with the jagged black rocks that lay in profusion everywhere between the various varieties of cactus. He unscrewed the cap.

"Do the same," he said.

"When we gonna drink, for crissakes?" Wagner demanded. "Gimme the machete! I'll do it!"

Slocum stared at Wagner. Then he shrugged and smiled. He handed the machete to Wagner. Wagner kneeled down. He jabbed the point in the thick outer skin of the cactus in three places, as if he were making a test plug in a watermelon to see if it was ripe. He pulled out the chunk and pressed his mouth against the cactus, as if a faucet were about to burst forth with water.

Nothing came out. After several seconds, Wagner cursed in his usual sullen fashion. He stood up.

"Gonna listen?" Slocum asked.

Without looking at Slocum, Wagner finally nodded.

"Prop up your canteen."

When he had finally done so with his usual rain of muttered curses, Slocum took off his shirt.

"What're you, goin' crazy with the heat?" Wagner shouted.

Slocum laid the shirt out flat on the ground. He held out his hand and waited patiently. Wagner slapped the machete into it.

Slocum lopped off the top of the cactus with one swift stroke. Then he ran the machete vertically around the inner edge. Next, he quickly sliced up the interior into fist-sized chunks. These he dropped unto the middle of his shirt. He brought the four corners of the shirt together, then twisted and twisted the ends until the pressure of the squeezing forced the water out of the pulp. It began to drip into the canteen.

Wagner said grudgingly, "That's pretty smart."

Slocum paid no attention. When his canteen was filled, he handed the machete to Wagner. While Wagner worked away to fill his own canteen, Slocum took the time to test-fire the Winchester.

He moistened a handful of dirt in the wet pulp and plastered the mud in an eight-inch circle on a barrel cactus. He paced off fifty feet. Any engagement in which he would be involved would very likely be at that distance or somewhat less.

The first bullet struck two o'clock on the outer edge of the target. By the third and last bullet he had corrected: it struck dead center. Satisfied, he walked back. Wagner was still squeezing away.

"Finished wastin' cartridges?"

Slocum shrugged. He had, after all, recently reminded himself that all he had to do was to put up with the stupid bastard for another week. He tore off a piece from the tail of his shirt—he had hung it over a dead cactus to dry while he sighted in—and, using a dead twig for a ramrod, he cleaned the carbine barrel as best he could. Even that brief exposure to the sun had burned his back slightly pink.

Their route next took them through an area of mesquite. Slocum stopped and picked several handfuls of the screw-shaped bean pods. As usual, Wagner was reluctant to try anything he considered, with contempt, to be Indian food. But he finally tried it and grudgingly admitted that the crisp, nutlike flavor was not so bad.

After he had eaten the beans, Wagner felt in a better mood. They followed an old deer trail that led them across the dull black lava rock. Slocum would not have ventured onto that baking hot surface if they did not have full canteens. The lava surface was made up of angular, sharpedged rocks and boulders with nothing but the flat, cracked black surface for miles. There was no sign of any kind of vegetation. Although the volcanic eruption had taken place millions of years before, the rainfall was still too sparse to weather away the rocks and form a primitive soil in which windblown seeds could lodge and sprout. The heat absorbed by the rock radiated upward through their boot soles. As soon as the sweat reached the surface of the skin it was instantaneously vaporized in the hundred and thirty degree heat. Their skins always felt dry to the touch.

The four Apaches, with their supplies of water and food looted from the miner's cabin, had made good time along a canyon that paralleled Slocum's course.

Alchisay looked down into the desert. He saw where the lava bed ended. Ahead there was a notch in the range, slightly to the left of the Belighannas' obvious route to Mexico. Up there, as any intelligent desert traveller would assume, there might be a *tinaja*. And if there was water in the tinaja, it would attract deer. That was where an Apache would go for food and water, and Alchisay, who had seen the mescal oven and, later, what Slocum had done with the barrel cactus, assumed that this Belighanna would do the same. Not like those two stupid ones he had just killed.

Craft would be required for a successful ambush. The Springfield was a powerful weapon, and Alchisay knew how to use it. That is, he could load and fire it, but he did not know how to use the sights. He knew that this was a kind of magic he did not have. So he would have to get very close to the Belighanna in order to kill him.

But *this* Belighanna, like an Apache, would very likely

notice anything out of the ordinary. He was sure to be extra wary in any place where the trail would run between cliffs. In such an area there would be no place for Alchisay to hide close enough so that he could fire the Springfield at point-blank range. And, for that first shot to be effective, Alchisay had better be really *close*. The center of the chest would have to be the target, and Alchisay would like to be no farther than thirty feet away. The big Springfield cartridge, almost the size of an asparagus stalk, packed enormous power. If it hit a man's chest, it would blow it wide apart. If he lived after that, so much the better; he would provide an hour's entertainment.

The other one was no problem.

Alchisay's stump throbbed. An angry red tinge had developed around the palm at the site of the amputation. The hand was beginning to swell with the coming of infection. It hurt. He wondered how long the big Belighanna would last staked out on the desert floor before he began to scream.

He pointed his chin at the notch in the range. "We go up there," he said.

They began to trot at the ground-eating pace of Apaches. Alchisay was not worried about losing liquid due to sweating. When he had killed the miner's horse, he had pulled out its intestines and squeezed them clean. Next, he had filled them with water. He made Nantije wrap them around his torso. There was enough water for all of them for three days.

Alchisay found a wide boulder with a dense growth of chaparral on one side of it. It was forty feet above the trail. He was pleased. The chaparral, first of all, would screen him from anyone who would glance upward. Sitting beside the boulder, he called Nantije over. He made a paste with water and dust and rubbed this mud over all the metal parts of the Springfield. Now no betraying glint would reveal its presence to a suspicious glance from the trail.

Still, that was not enough. The glossy walnut of the stock did not blend well with the light tan color which was the dominant hue of the chaparral. So he next rubbed mud over the stock. He held it out in the full glare of the sun for thirty seconds. The violent, searing heat dried it almost instantly. Satisfied, he set it down carefully. Then he walked through the chaparral. Nantije had taken off the horse intestine. He stood sullenly in the woman's long brown dress.

Ditoh handed Nantije the sunbonnet. Nantije stared at it in distaste.

Ditoh prodded him in the ribs and growled, "Put it on!"

Nantije did so reluctantly. Alchisay stared at him critically. With his face shadowed by the sunbonnet's visor he looked all right, Alchisay decided. But his big brown hands gave him away. Alchisay frowned. Delchay had a solution. He had noticed a clump of Mormon tea nearby. Pioneer women, following Indian custom, brewed a refreshing drink by steeping its stems in boiling water.

It would be a natural thing for a woman to be carrying a bunch of the stuff home. And Nantije's big brown hands would be nicely concealed in the mass of branches.

The two Belighanna would be so absorbed in staring at the sudden appearance of a white woman in this wilderness, where they had never expected to see one, that their attention would be drawn away from Alchisay's ambush position.

Delchay thought that Nantije looked very funny. He kept saying things like "You are very pretty" and "Would you sleep with me tonight?" He said, "How many horses does your father want for you?" Nantije got angrier and angrier. Finally Alchisay had to step between them and tell them both to shut up. He was annoyed that it was Nantije who first noticed the two Belighanna; Alchisay was the one who should have seen them first.

The tall one was in front. He carried the Winchester in a loose, relaxed, but competent way that showed he knew how to use it. The other one followed, a few steps behind. Alchisay was sure that if the man were alone he would not survive one hour in Apache country. He looked only at the trail. Alchisay climbed up to his position beside the boulder. He picked up the Springfield. Ditoh took up his position. Nantije waited for Alchisay's signal to start walking.

The tall one's head never stopped moving. This was an ideal ambush spot. Slocum looked at the ridgetop, then up and down the sides of the narrow valley. His gaze scanned the boulder behind which Alchisay was hiding, but his camouflage was so expert that Slocum's look skimmed past the Springfield. Alchisay grinned. The tall one's stare drifted across the chaparral. Alchisay trilled a cardinal's high note. Nantije immediately began walking down the trail.

When he had gone a few paces, Alchisay suddenly realized that Nantije was wearing his moccasins. He cursed, but there was nothing he could do about it now.

Slocum wanted to examine the valley slopes more intensely. He waved Wagner past him. Wagner went ahead, carrying the machete. He was first around a bend in the trail. He stopped short in amazement at the sight of a white woman in this wilderness. She was calmly carrying a big bunch of Mormon tea in her arms as if she had just stepped out of the corner general store.

Slocum noticed that Wagner had stopped. He brought up the carbine and moved cautiously up the trail.

"Jesus! A woman!" Wagner said. He added, "Howdy, ma'am."

She did not respond. She continued to walk steadily

toward them. Alchisay had already thrust the block home. He sighted through the V-notch at Slocum's chest.

A sixth sense warned Slocum that something was wrong. A white woman in this situation would have stopped short. She would have been wary; she would have tried to analyze the strangers. She was facing the sun. Even though her sunbonnet had a visor, she should have brought up a palm to shade her eyes even more against that white, ferocious glare, in order to see better. She would have responded with a cautious "Howdy! Who mought you be?" Or she would have responded with some sort of a greeting, however brief, to Wagner's greeting. That was the frontier custom.

But this woman kept silent. She kept walking, like a machine. Slocum overtook Wagner. He pushed the man forcefully to one side. This was no time for good manners. He wanted a fast look at this phenomenon.

Wagner started to utter a pained complaint. But Nantije was sure that he was about to be discovered. Slocum was ten feet from him and clearly about to come even closer. Nantije's knife was in his right hand, which was buried inside the bunch of Mormon tea. Nantije suddenly dropped the Mormon tea, took one big step—which was hampered by the dress—and then hurled himself at Slocum, with his knife arm upraised.

The sudden, unplanned move spoiled Alchisay's aim. For just as Nantije launched himself Alchisay fired. As the Springfield bellowed in the narrow valley, Slocum fired from the hip. His bullet entered Nantije's left shoulder, broke his collarbone, ranged downward, and blew his heart apart. He was dead when he hit the ground.

Alchisay's slug smashed against the right side of Slocum's head. It continued, slammed against the carbine's firing mechanism, ruined it, ricocheted against a boulder, and then went screaming across the lava beds.

Slocum fell, unconscious. Wagner took one horrified look, saw the Apaches standing up in the chaparral, and, bending down, grabbed the carbine. He did not know that it was damaged beyond repair. He spun and ran away from the Apaches and downhill the way he had come. Fear and excitement made him run like a jackrabbit.

Alchisay fed in another cartridge and fired. The sound of the heavy explosion made Wagner run ever faster. Ditoh started after him.

"Stop!" Alchisay shouted. He had seen Slocum move. With Nantije dead, Alchisay did not want to risk losing Ditoh to a man who had a carbine. Besides, the man had no water, there was no water and no wells in the direction he was going, across the lava beds; so they could pick him up tomorrow, when he would be dying of thirst.

Alchisay came down the slope. He stood over the prostrate Slocum. Just beyond lay the dead Nantije. Slocum began to stir. Good; he would be conscious that evening when Alchisay would take revenge for Nantije.

"Tie him," he said.

When Ditoh had finished tying Slocum, Alchisay tested the rawhide. Ditoh didn't like that, and frowned. Delchay, who was Nantije's second cousin, was furious at the boy's death. He blamed it on Alchisay's idea of disguising him as a woman. But he said nothing. Alchisay's rages were unpleasant, and now that his hand was aching he was worse than ever.

"I said, 'Didn't you listen?'"

"What?" Delchay said, startled. He hadn't listened to what Alchisay had just said.

Alchisay gritted, "Get some cholla needles. Stick them in a beaver-tail pad."

"What for?"

"Get them," Alchisay repeated. He swung the muzzle of the Springfield around till it faced Delchay.

Delchay reluctantly began searching.

When he was out of hearing, Ditoh asked Delchay's question. They had been friends for a long time, whereas Nantije and Delchay were relatively recent acquaintances.

"You will see," Alchisay said with a hard grin. He began to look under mesquite bushes and wherever there might be shade. For, until the midday heat would dissipate, that was where the cold-blooded reptiles stayed.

Especially the poisonous Gila monsters. Within five minutes he found a big one.

12

Wagner ran down a dry wash, stumbling in his blind panic. His head down, he pumped his arms in the style of a long-distance runner in an attempt to get up more speed. He had never run so fast in his life, not even when he was a boy playing hide-and-seek with the children of the Mexican *vaqueros* who worked for his father.

Now he was playing hide-and-seek for real.

When the wash swung to the left to avoid a massive hard lava cliff, Wagner halted. He was panting in heaving gasps and he dripped with sweat. He crept to the top of a ridge. Next, imitating Slocum, he picked a bunch of *jojoba*. He removed his sombrero and placed the *jojoba* at the ridge crest. Then he peered through the stems.

He saw a mile up the wash. He saw nothing except scattered clumps of cactus and some sparse grass interspersed among the boulders that had been rounded by eons of wear by the spring rains.

Wagner began to relax. His frantic breathing started to slow down. He had shed his canteen in his wild run. He had no idea where he had flung the machete aside. In his panic he didn't want to be encumbered by anything except the carbine. Then he looked at it and realized with a despairing sensation that it was no good.

He was sure that Slocum was dead. Earlier that day when he had asked Slocum where they were heading, the grim face had relaxed enough to say, "Puerto Peñasco."

"Never heard of it," Wagner said in a complaining tone.

"Well, isn't that just peachy," Slocum said in that ironic tone Wagner hated. "If Mr. Russell Wagner never heard of it I guess it doesn't exist. Or if it did, it oughta to be ashamed of itself." Wagner resented that remark. He asked no more questions. But when he thought about it, it was the tall green-eyed man who had planned their prison escape, carried it through, and then got them this far across a grim, forbidding desert.

And then to be killed by an Apache disguised as a woman!

It was ironic. Wagner shook his head. Secretly, a part of him was pleased that the man who had continually nagged and insulted him was dead. But, on the other hand, the man had certain skills. He ought to be emulated. If Slocum wanted to go to Puerto Peñasco, he probably knew what he was doing. Wagner decided to head there.

Slocum had taught him how to extract water from barrel cactus. He had taught him that mesquite pods were nourishing. And he had taught him to move at night in the desert country in order to conserve water.

So Wagner now felt he had a chance. During the day, he decided, he would head south along the ridges, where it was cooler. At night, if he had enough energy left, he would descend to the desert and search for barrel cactus. He was under the impression that it could be found everywhere. But he would always make sure that he was trending south. He began to feel confident that he could do it just as well as Slocum. He turned.

No Apaches were visible. He began walking.

And then it struck like a lightning flash: the Apaches were not following because they had Slocum. And therefore Slocum was still alive, because they were torturing him; they would rather do that than look for Wagner.

Because, if Slocum were dead, the Apaches would be right on top of Wagner, because of the obvious trail he had left. Wagner halted and thought. Should he go back and try to save Slocum? The thought made him shudder. The Apaches had knives and a Springfield rifle. The odds were too heavy. Tough shit, John.

He continued to walk south.

Alchisay held up the Gila monster. One massive brown hand gripped the thick, muscular neck. The other hand held the tail firmly, in spite of its contractions in its attempt to escape. From its blunt nose to the tip of its tail, the reptile's black and orange pattern extended thirty inches.

It writhed in powerful, convulsive shudders that took all of Alchisay's strength to control. Its mouth gaped wide open as its sharp, poisonous fangs sought to clamp the enemy's hands. It hissed violently.

Ditoh stepped back a respectful distance. He was very nervous about snakes and poisonous lizards. When he was four, a rattler had struck his right arm as he bent down to pick up an arrow he had just shot from his child's bow. He still remembered the excitement as his mother searched frantically for jimson weed.

She finally found some and made a poultice from it. His

arm turned black and swelled up to four times its normal size, but finally, after about ten days, he was all right. But he still remembered how much the poison had made his arm hurt.

The Gila monster hissed furiously. Its mouth was fully open and its ugly head twisted from side to side as it sought a target. The clear yellow fluid of its virulent poison began to dribble down from its fixed fangs.

Ditoh stepped back another pace.

Slocum opened his eyes. His head ached violently from the glancing sledge-hammer blow of the heavy slug from the Springfield. Then he saw the writhing lizard.

He turned his head from side to side. Wagner was not in sight, so he had either been killed or had escaped. Probably the former, Slocum thought. Slocum did not think much of Wagner's abilities to survive. Slocum's tightly bound hands dug into the small of his back in a painful fashion.

His legs were free. While Slocum began to think that it would be a good idea to get up and make a run for it, two of the Apaches suddenly approached. They pulled off one boot, and then jerked the pants off that leg. Then they drove two sharpened pegs deep into the hard soil with rocks. Next, they lashed Slocum's ankles to the pegs so tightly that movement was impossible. Slocum cursed. If he had regained consciousness a minute earlier, he might have escaped.

Now he lay spread-eagled, naked from the waist down. Under the small of his back there pressed a sharp little rock that promised good results if no one noticed what he would be attempting.

Slocum slid down three inches. This movement bent his knees somewhat, but it was not noticed. Now his wrists were jammed against the top, the cutting edge, of the rock. Very slowly, with as much pressure as he could, he began to rub them against the sharp edge. It was hard to do, with the full weight of his torso on his hands. A braided rope, Slocum knew, would announce its dissolution by the strands parting one by one. A rawhide would give no warning whatsoever that anything was happening.

Dusk came with the dramatic speed of the desert sunset. Ditoh made a small fire. Alchisay held the sullenly struggling and hissing Gila monster. Slocum did not understand why the stocky, ugly Apache was holding the goddamn thing. Then Ditoh picked up the broad, thick leaf of the beavertail cactus. He had bunched up a few strands of grass and brushed away the spines. He showed the leaf to Alchisay. Alchisay nodded, while still giving every effort to control the angry Gila monster. It was becoming more furious by the second.

Slocum watched with fascinated interest while he worked his wrists up and down. He was glad that the reptile held the stares of the Apaches; that meant that they did not look at him as he worked his wrists back and forth. Had they noticed, they would have become suspicious and investigated.

The reptile was amazingly strong. Alchisay's forearm muscles bulged as he strained to hold it while Ditoh, following instructions, jabbed his knife into its belly a quarter of an inch.

Slocum hoped they would keep on torturing the poor lizard. They were still so fascinated in what Slocum took to be some sort of vicious little amusement that no attention was yet being paid to their prisoner. He took every advantage of this and increased his rubbing against the rock.

Finally Alchisay was satisfied. The enraged Gila monster would produce plenty of venom. Alchisay watched while Ditoh gingerly shoved the beavertail pad into the reptile's jaws.

The sharp fangs clamped down on what the Gila monster

was fully convinced was the enemy responsible for its agony. The venom dribbled copiously into the cactus flesh. The ugly jaws gripped like a bulldog. Every time its jaws shifted for a better grip, Ditoh nervously moved the cactus pad so that all of it would become saturated with poison.

Finally Alchisay said, "Enough. Where is the *cholla?*" Ditoh held another beavertail pad. He had rubbed it against the *cholla,* and hundreds of the tiny, viciously barbed spines now clung to the beavertail.

As soon as Slocum saw Ditoh carefully insert a *cholla,* he knew what was going to happen. It was why they had exposed his genitals. They were going to insert the poisoned spines into his penis.

Slocum rubbed his wrists even more quickly. He felt the stone gouging into his flesh. It didn't matter. He felt blood sliding down from the raw flesh.

Suddenly the rawhide parted. Slocum gasped in relief. He flexed his hands and fingers as hard as he could to encourage the circulation to return. They were numb.

He knew he could not use them as weapons for quite some time. He could not even grab the knife which he saw in Ditoh's belt, only two feet from him. He was as helpless as a baby. He flexed his hands to strengthen them.

Ditoh picked up a spine. He held it between two big brown fingers and turned toward Slocum.

Alchisay bent over still more so that he could watch Slocum's face as the spine went in. He unconsciously slackened his grip on the Gila monster's neck. As Alchisay's face neared the reptile's gaping mouth, it suddenly wrenched itself loose and struck at the Apache's face.

The teeth locked into Alchisay's upper lip on the left side. Alchisay let out a startled cry and straightened up suddenly. He tried to pull it away.

Ditoh was startled at the exclamation made by Alchisay. He stood up and took a step toward Alchisay. He tripped over the peg to which Slocum's left ankle was attached. He fell face downward into the fire, which was by now a big one.

He yelled in surprise and pain. As he twisted, trying to escape the flames, he scattered the fire. The light it had given disappeared, except for a few small patches. The Gila monster had locked onto Alchisay's lip with bulldog tenacity. He was desperately trying to jerk it loose. He yelled for Ditoh to cut it from him with his knife, but Ditoh was in agony from his burns. Delchay was paralyzed and couldn't think clearly.

Everything was perfect for departure, Slocum decided. He sat up. Enough strength had come back to his hands so that he could slide the ankle thongs up until they cleared the tops of the pegs. None of the Apaches could see him any more, because the fire had gone out. Moreover, they were so busy with Alchisay's problem that none of them were looking in his direction. He quickly felt around in the darkness for the Springfield; he had last seen it in back of Alchisay.

But Ditoh had now scrambled to his feet, and with an angry look at Delchay, who was still frozen in awe at the sight of the Gila monster—he thought that Slocum was a sorcerer and had commanded the lizard—he began to hack away at the Gila monster with his knife. He gripped the tail in his left hand and began sawing at the massive neck.

The immediate effect was to make the reptile exert more pressure upon Alchisay's lip. The fire began to flare up.

Slocum decided not to waste any more time looking for the Springfield. Even if he found it, he wouldn't be able to use it right now, and if they did see him, one of them knew where it was and could use it, while the other one could come at him with the knife.

Time to go.

Slocum turned and melted quietly into the darkness. He could move as silently as an Apache when he chose. As he moved away, he heard the moaning and cursing of Alchisay and Ditoh, one suffering painful burns over his face, chest, and belly, and the other with a Gila monster clinging to his upper lip.

He was two hundred yards away when Ditoh finally severed the head. But it still clung to Alchisay's face like a grotesque wart. Alchisay tugged it with fury. It finally broke away. Within its jaws was the left half of Alchisay's upper lip.

Alchisay flung the head away with rage. It was then that he realized that Slocum had vanished. Alchisay stood and raged helplessly while the blood dribbled down his jaw. Ditoh busied himself starting a fire. Both Ditoh and Delchay stared at the mutilated face.

"He is a sorcerer," Delchay said in awe.

"You are a fool!" Alchisay yelled.

Delchay hunkered down and removed the still good pieces of rawhide. He coiled them up. He did not like being insulted.

Alchisay said, his voice sounding strange because of the lip, "We will start after him at first light."

Ditoh looked down. His chest and belly were covered with huge white blisters. He rocked back and forth in pain.

"Rest now," Alchisay said.

"How?" Ditoh asked. Delchay let out a short, ironic laugh. Ditoh placed both hands over his chest. The pain was increasing. Alchisay gingerly touched his lip. A thick blood clot had formed on the torn flesh.

Alchisay began to think. One white man without weapons, and with his genitals swollen with poison, could not cover much distance. Once the three Apaches caught up with the Belighanna there was nothing that he could do, clever as he was. Not when the Apaches had a Colt, a Springfield, and knives, and were desert-cunning.

"Rest," Alchisay said, and glared at them. No one said anything. "We will get him tomorrow and finish the job."

13

As Slocum stumbled on in the dark, he kept opening and closing his fists. When he had gone about two miles, he figured, the sensation had come back to them.

There was one thing that made him feel better: the realization that two of the Apaches were suffering as well. They would not, moreover, follow in the dark. Apaches were too fearful of old enemy ghosts. The ghosts moved only at night as they sought to bring sickness and bad luck to whoever had angered them when they were alive.

But as soon as the sky lightened, they would be after him. He needed food, weapons, and a defensible position. He needed medicine. The chances of finding any one of these in the dark was impossible.

All he could do was keep moving.

And even then he could not make good time. Not through the scrub chaparral, with small rocks over which he would continually stumble.

The Apaches had planned to drive in close to a hundred spines. The total amount of poison would then have been just about equal to a full-scale bite. The fact that the big Apache had gotten bitten was what had saved Slocum. Because they had wanted something special in the way of torture, that had ultimately been his salvation. If they had gone about the traditional method of torture, nothing would have happened to the two Apaches. So, in a sense, Slocum felt he should be grateful to the Gila monster.

He felt a little better when he thought about that. But he was suddenly very thirsty and very hungry. He had forgotten when he had drunk and eaten last. He was exhausted. Yet to stop and rest, which he needed very badly, would set the Apaches on his trail within an hour after sunrise.

He plodded grimly on.

Wagner, in spite of his newly won confidence about desert survival, was to find out that it was not as easy as it looked.

For a while he felt sure that the desert would be a big general store. It would supply him with food and drink. *Chia* seeds were edible; so were cattail roots and *jojoba* nuts. *Toyon* berries could be eaten raw. And water could be squeezed from barrel cactus. It all seemed so easy.

After a chilly night, which he spent shivering with his back against a *sahuaro*, he woke up when a cactus wren chirped above his head as it entered its nest. He searched for barrel cactus. His tongue felt wooly and thick in his mouth, and there was no saliva. When he found one, he told himself, he knew just what to do; Slocum had taught him. In fifteen minutes after he found one, he would be drinking at least a pint of slightly astringent but completely palatable water. So he thought.

The problem was that there were no barrel cactus to be found.

Nor did he see any mesquite; and he had planned to munch some of its nutlike pods. In his disconsolate prowlings around a small outwash plain that debouched out into the desert from one of the narrow canyons of the range, he brushed against a *cholla*. He paused with an angry curse to dig out the spines, which had settled on his skin as gently as smoke.

While he stood in the already suffocating heat he execrated the desert, the *cholla,* and Slocum for dragging him there. His mouth was drier than before. Even putting in a little pebble was no use. "You goddamn son of a bitch!" he kept repeating over and over, until he realized that it took energy. And energy was what he needed right now. He shut up.

Ironically, at that very moment, while he was also suffering the pangs of *cholla,* Slocum had found an arroyo with a dense thicket of *chamisa* against one cliff. The *chamisa* had sprung up among a mass of small boulders. Slocum heaved two of the boulders aside. Underneath, the ground was damp. He kneeled and began to dig with a sharp branch. The soil became damper. Excited, he now dug with his hands, paying no attention to the fact that he was scraping the backs of his fingers raw. Soon the damp soil became muddy. Six more inches, which took fifteen minutes, and ground water began to trickle in.

While he waited for the water to seep in with agonizing slowness, he searched the hillsides for milkweed. He must have passed plenty during the night, but he never would have been able to see it.

He found a clump growing on the far side of the *chamisa*. He pulled up three of the low-growing plants and broke off the roots. He pounded them between two stones till they were crushed flat.

The pit was almost full of water. It was muddy, but it was cool. He shook a few drops onto a flat rock and then bent over and smelled. It did not have any vile chemical aroma. It was safe.

The flavor was sweet. He drank slowly, taking his time between swallows. When he finished, he placed the milk-weed roots in the pit and waited for them to absorb the water. He stood up and walked painfully to a Spanish bayonet nearby. He pulled a leaf from it, tore the leaf vertically a few times till he had several of the strong white fibers.

As he turned to go down the slope he saw three tiny brown specks in the far distance. He waddled down the slope as quickly as he could. He took out the wet roots and wrapped them around his genitals. He tied them firmly into place with the bayonet fibers and pulled his pants on again. Next, he lay flat and drank as much as his stomach could hold. He moved the boulders back into place and rubbed away his tracks around the water hole with a clump of *chamisa* branches. Let the goddamn Chiricahuas find their own water. He thanked God for the milkweed. The poultice began lessening the pain and the inflammation within minutes. He had to move, and fast.

Instead of finding shade and holing up till dark, Wagner kept moving on, looking for water. He was past coherent thinking now. The water content of his blood was fast disappearing in the form of sweat. The blood, as a result, became thicker and thicker. His heart was forced to pump extra hard in order to push the blood through his arteries.

Wagner could actually feel it pumping in a jerky, labored fashion. He needed energy from some sort of food—*any* food—and he wasn't getting it. His legs could no longer support his weight easily. He began to stumble over low clumps of bear grass. His body refused to obey his brain's instructions to walk around the obstacle. His mouth no longer could produce any saliva. His tongue began to swell even more. It was the first stage of death by thirst.

The milkweed poultice had worked a miracle. The redness and swelling had almost disappeared; the pain had gone completely. Slocum began to take longer strides, in spite of his weakness. He had to find a place where he could be safe.

Ditoh went first. Ordinarily Delchay would have taken that function, but he had quietly left that morning. It was the right of anyone in a war party to do so, and he had simply said, "I'm going home."

When Alchisay pressed him for a reason he simply said, "The Gila monster is a sorcerer; he will come again." Alchisay tried to persuade him to stay; he said, "You will not get any money!"

Delchay said, "What good would money be to a man who is bewitched?"

And so Alchisay tried once more. He said, "What about the pass from the agent?"

Delchay said nothing; it was clear that he considered facing a sorcerer a more terrible fate than being caught off the reservation without a pass.

It was Ditoh's function as a scout to draw enemy fire— if there was any—and so force the enemy to reveal his location and strength. If that should happen, Alchisay would be ready with his Springfield. He had no intention of killing Slocum. That is, not right away. It would happen after the Belighanna had spent a long time wishing he were dead. Alchisay had a missing finger and lip to avenge; Ditoh had his painful burns, which he well knew would leave his chest and belly scarred badly for life.

So both of them were extraordinarily intent on tracking Slocum. There was no way Slocum could conceal his trail in this stretch. The desert and uplands were littered with dried twigs, ant burrows, and windblown dust. Tracing was as easy as if he had posted a notice every few feet.

Ditoh said, "Here he stopped and did something. I don't know what." This was the place where Slocum had pulled on his pants.

Alchisay said curtly, "He pissed."

Ditoh took the remark seriously. He looked around to see if the urine, which would have vaporized almost as quickly as if the desert floor were a stove-lid, had left a series of tiny craters in the dust. There were none. Ditoh said seriously, "No. He stopped for something else. He—"

Then he noticed Alchisay's grin. The exposed upper canine gave him an extraordinarily wolfish look. For a second Ditoh actually thought that the spirit of a wolf might have entered Alchisay's soul. He tried to thrust the thought from him. But one never knew. So, instead of a furious response, he contented himself with a shrug.

He continued. "Afterwards, he began to take longer steps. You see?"

Alchisay's face was throbbing violently. "Of course I see!" he snapped. "Keep going."

Ditoh hid his resentment. No wonder Delchay had left, he thought. He resumed his tracking.

Wagner no longer knew what he was doing. He stumbled over a beavertail cactus. As he struggled painfully to his knees his lacerated hands fell against the fleshy pads. Their soft feel suggested moisture. He grabbed one and crammed it into his mouth. He did not care about the spines. He chewed the pulp and spat it out. There was a damp sensation on his tongue which was worth the pain of having the spines driven into his tongue and cheeks. Encouraged, he sank to his knees and broke off another pad. He began to chew. Now he felt the pain of the spines. He moaned and kept chewing. He no longer cared about anything as trivial as pain.

They were better fed than he was. It was only a matter of half an hour or so before they closed in on him. The only thing Slocum could think of in this area of cliffs and narrow arroyos would be to lure them into some sort of passageway. He hoped to find such an ideal ambuscade; then he would race ahead, weak though he was, climb up to the cliff edge looking down at them, and then shove several huge boulders over the rim.

But he recognized this as a crazy fantasy.

The cliffs were too high, first of all. Secondly, there didn't seem to be any handholds. And, even if there were any, his weakened hands simply could not take his weight for the climb to the top. If he tried it, he would have to take frequent rests. And during one of those rests the big Apache with the Springfield would appear. He would look up at Slocum. Then he would grin with that ugly face of his. And then he would very carefully aim and fire. If Slocum had any luck at that time it would be if the Chiricahua shot him in the heart. Otherwise the Apaches would stretch out his dying for a very long time, whether he suffered a broken leg or arm in the fall. Whatever happened, it would be the end of John Slocum, dead in a lonely arroyo in the most desolate desert of Arizona.

• • •

"I see him!"

Ditoh pointed. Alchisay looked. He saw the tiny figure disappear between two rock cliffs.

"Good," he said. "Very good." He pulled the bolt back and dropped the huge Springfield cartridge into the chamber, then slammed the bolt shut. It gave off the fine metallic click that he liked. There was no other sound like it. It might be necessary to kill the man instead of taking him prisoner. If that happened, they could defile the corpse so that its spirit would never find happiness in the afterlife.

But at least they would have the Belighanna's head.

Wagner had made surprisingly good time in his southerly flight. Slocum would never have believed him capable of it. Fear had given wings to his feet. He was now circling around the base of the range which Slocum was penetrating in his attempt to find a defensible position.

With neither one having any knowledge of the other's course, both were roughly parallel. Wagner was on the desert floor; Slocum was moving up the arroyo, two miles inside the range.

Wagner's tongue had now swollen to twice its normal size, partly because of his thirst, and partly because the spines embedded in it had infected the tissue.

He was heedless. All he cared about was water. He thought of a waterfall he had seen in the Mogollones once. He had passed it by with only a casual stare, as if it were of no importance. How stupid he had been; it was the most important thing in the world! He cursed himself now because he had not dismounted, lain flat, and drunk that cold, clear water until he could not squeeze any more inside his belly. He started to cry.

A few minutes later, he decided it was too hot to wear

a hat. He threw the sombrero away. It was getting too heavy anyway.

Slocum started a jog-trot. He needed the extra distance he would gain by the faster pace in order to contrive or plan an adequate defense. But he saw nothing. *Nothing*. Not even a straight branch of anything that he could sharpen on a rock and so produce a makeshift spear. With a spear he could get behind a boulder, wait till the scout neared, and lunge at him. With luck he might actually get him in the belly. Then, with luck, he might get the man's knife. Then—

But there was nothing. No branch. No boulder. Just the vertical cliffs and the sandy, meandering streambed which was full of melt water in the spring. One mile back, he saw the scout move into sight.

Slocum turned and went on at his jog-trot. He didn't think that a starving man could have done such a thing, but he pulled upon deep reserves, which he did not even suspect that he possessed. He was losing water through this violent exertion. He could not see any alternative. His heart was pounding with heavy thuds, as if trying to tear itself loose from his rib cage.

Wagner saw a four-foot-long diamondback rattlesnake. It did not live in the desert, it preferred higher and cooler elevations. It had followed a rabbit scent during the night, struck, killed, and eaten it. It was waiting patiently in the shade of a mesquite for cooler temperatures before it went back.

To Wagner the snake meant food and liquid. Without a second's hesitation, he fell on it. His left hand gripped it just behind its head. The right hand grasped the tail with its rattles.

He lifted the rattler and bit a piece from its middle. A four-foot-long diamondback has powerful muscles. It convulsed in its struggle to break free. Wagner did not know where his strength came from. The tail writhed and vibrated. Wagner paid no attention to the ominous sound, like dried peas rattling in a pod. He took another bite. He remembered that Slocum had told him that rattlesnake tasted like chicken.

"I bet the bastard never ate a rattler raw," Wagner said aloud. He laughed and took another bite. By now the snake was dead. He ate another bite from the neck. Then he wrenched off the triangular head with its unblinking yellow eyes and threw it away.

He felt stronger. Liquid oozed out of the body cavity. He lifted the snake and licked. He rolled what was left and shoved it into his shirt. He began walking. He noticed that his steps were longer.

"I ain't gonna tell *nobody* 'bout this," he mumbled. "They'd never let me into their house no more. *Ever!*"

He began to laugh, and he could not stop.

On the vertical cliff to his left, Slocum saw a narrow ledge. He estimated it to be two feet wide. It began at ground level and angled upward at a twenty-degree slope till it was fifty feet above him. At that point the ledge ended. But where it ended there was a two-foot-wide gap in the cliff. Slocum could not see into it from the ground where he was standing. But for him the essential thing was that it was higher than the trail.

He had learned the hard way, in the Civil War, that a very wise military axiom was: always seize the high ground.

So he walked up the ledge. When it broke to the left, he took one step and froze in astonishment.

Three hundred and thirty-eight years before, Don Pedro de Alarcón, the youngest son of a Spanish nobleman of Andalucia, had joined the expedition of Coronado.

Alarcón's father, who had fallen upon bad times, had given his son all the money he could spare. He had sold three hundred acres of his patrimony. He told his son to go and make his fortune in the New World, as so many younger sons were doing. Cortés and Pizarro had done so; why not Pedro de Alarcón? So Alarcón bought a fine sword and some good armor, both of which were very costly. He bought a superb war horse. Then he found passage on a galleon sailing out of Cadiz for San Juan de Ullua, which was later to be called Vera Cruz.

In Mexico City he met Coronado, who was looking for just such restless and well-armed men. Coronado was about to set forth on his expedition to seek the gold he believed could be found in the mythical Seven Cities of Cibola.

They set off to the north. Both men were arrogant. They disagreed on almost every issue. As they neared what was later to become the border between Mexico and the state of Arizona, de Alarcón had his final fight. He told Coronado to go to hell, and he split off with his twenty-three foot soldiers, eight men-at-arms, and his sixteen Mayo Indian slaves. The Mayos, who came from central Chihuahua, were along to carry supplies. There were twelve horses. The horsemen carried twelve-foot-long lances, which had proven to be very effective against Indian attackers.

De Alarcón next headed northwest. In that direction, said one of the Mayos—who hated the Spaniards—could be found Indian towns and even cities where the chiefs were almost bent double under the weight of their ceremonial gold necklaces. And, added the Mayo, when he saw the excitement in the Spaniard's eyes, they ate from golden plates.

Of course, the Mayo had invented the golden cities. He wanted that arrogant conquistador to die in his struggle to cross the Yuma Desert.

They ran into trouble right away. There was not enough grass for the horses. Deer were scanty that year. The men began to starve and wanted to go back. De Alarcón shot two of them for mutiny and grimly pushed on.

Water next began to be a problem. The Indians, who were suffering just as much as their masters, knew that there would probably be water in the *tinajas*, the water-filled pools in the mountains.

So, stumbling and cursing, like Wagner so many years later, they struggled along the trail into the range. One of the men-at-arms, a certain Santiago Ruiz, was the first man to notice the two-foot ledge. He shouted that there was probably water in there.

De Alarcón and the rest of the expedition followed him.

They saw a box canyon. And where there had been a *tinaja* there was now a hollow, dusty granite bowl. There had been a five-year-long drought. That explained the sparse grass and the scarce deer.

In despair, de Alarcón dismounted. He sat with his back against the wall of the box canyon. The men-at-arms joined him, and so did the Mayos. They did not even bother to unsaddle the horses. Finally, the worn-out animals collapsed. The men watched them with dull eyes.

And in that place they died. All of them, the men and the horses. No one had seen them until the day Slocum stood at the entrance to the box canyon.

De Alarcón sat against the wall where he had fallen asleep so many years before. Because he was encased in armor, the *zapilotes* and coyotes had not touched him. The hot, dry air had mummified him. His shrivelled hand still held his sword. His helmet was in his lap. His legs were extended. His silver spurs were still attached to his boots.

Elsewhere, because the others had not worn any armor, skulls, thigh, rib, and arm bones lay in a confusing jumble, just where the coyotes had dragged them and gnawed the flesh from them. The skeletons of the horses were scrambled everywhere, in some places in a neat pile, in other areas scattered like a game of jackstraws. Slocum had never seen anything like it. A strange silence lay over the field of bones. Slocum felt a shiver of awe ripple through him. The only sound was the wind whistling as it blew overhead.

But there was no time to savor the terrible beauty of this place. The Chiricahuas were close behind. Slocum knew that they would spend only a brief time reconnoitering before they became bolder and entered the box canyon.

Slocum stripped quickly. De Alarcón had been unusually big for a Spaniard. Slocum bent down and unbuckled his chest cuirass. He unbuckled the leg greaves. He pulled on the boots, donned the armor, put on the helmet. He pulled down the visor. He tested the edge of the blade with his thumb. The dry air had protected the Toledo blade from rust or dulling. The edge was so sharp that a hairline of blood appeared on the ball of his thumb.

Satisfied, Slocum felt the point. It was equally sharp. He picked up one of the lances and placed its shaft close by. Then he sat down with his back against the rock cliff. With his legs thrust in front of him, he looked as if he were dead, like the man whose armor he now wore.

Ditoh was reluctant about entering the gap.

Alchisay stood below and looked up at him.

"Well?"

"He went up here," Ditoh said, staring at the dust on the ledge. "Then he went in."

"Well?" Alchisay repeated angrily. His face throbbed violently. The infection was getting worse. He wanted to get at the Belighanna, and quickly.

Apaches were realists as far as evaluating possible ambushes went. Concerning dead and vengeful spirits they could be as hysterical and jittery as a neurotic woman. But when it came to warfare and intelligent ways to conduct it on their own terrain, they were unbeatable.

Ditoh shrugged and pointed inside. "I can't see where it goes," he said. What he really dreaded was to have a boulder topple over on him from the top of the cliff.

"Find out!"

Ditoh said in a sullen manner, "I will, if you walk in beside me."

Alchisay considered. He was leading a war party, as it were. Warriors enlisted in war parties, but Apache war parties were different from white warfare. A man enlisted in the U. S. Cavalry. Once he signed up, it was made very clear that if he did not take orders from his superiors the penalty ranged, from prison in peacetime to execution in wartime.

With Apaches, a commander could give orders. They were obeyed as long as they were considered reasonable or successful. As soon as an Apache warrior decided that the orders were ridiculous, or doomed to failure because of superior strength or sorcery, he was free to walk away, with no blame attached. No one would think the worse of him. He simply said, "The leader had bad medicine."

Both Ditoh and Alchisay knew that this event was trembling on the brink. If Alchisay wanted to remain the leader, he would have to yield.

"All right," he said, after a moment's hesitation. "I'll go in with you."

When he finally had climbed the ledge and was standing beside Ditoh, he grabbed Ditoh's elbow just as the man was about to start.

"And I'll go *first*," he said contemptuously.

That was not the point of Ditoh's complaint at all. He had simply wanted another pair of eyes to help his scouting before he entered such a dangerous ambuscade area.

And now Ditoh began to think angrily about what would happen when they returned to San Carlos. Alchisay would go around telling everyone how scared Ditoh had been. And when some war chief next announced that he was seeking volunteers for a war party, Ditoh would be rejected.

He was furious, and he lost no time telling Alchisay the reasons why. They were yelling at each other in rage as they entered the box canyon.

Slocum had enough warning. He stood up and leaned against the rock wall. He stuck the sword in its scabbard and made sure it would draw easily. He grabbed the lance with both hands and froze rigidly. Sweat began to drip under his cuirass and helmet.

The two Chiricahuas entered the place of bones together.

Wagner caught a small brown lizard. It had relied upon its color for camouflage when it congealed against a dead, brown *saguaro* stump as Wagner neared.

But Wagner's eyesight had sharpened enormously lately. His peripheral vision had seen the minuscule flicker of the lizard just before it became motionless.

Wagner's swollen hand, inflamed by cactus spines, shot out and grabbed the lizard. He snapped its neck and bit. He stuck it into his right shirt pocket. There it joined three more dead lizards. He was saving them for supper.

Ditoh was the first one to see.

He stopped so abruptly that Alchisay, following him into the narrow canyon entrance, bumped into him. Alchisay's instinctive reaction was to step around Ditoh and bring the

Springfield into action; he thought that Ditoh had spotted the white man. Then he, too, saw.

It seemed perfectly natural that one skeleton in armor, with a helmet and visor down, should be leaning motionless against the rock wall ten feet to their left.

Alchisay slowly lowered the Springfield. There was nothing but death here, and a myriad of ghosts. His gaze travelled slowly across the field of bones. Their ghosts were poised, and ready to leap into their souls.

"Look," Ditoh whispered. He pointed. The Belighanna's tracks ended in the middle of the tangle of skulls and ribs and horses' skeletons.

"And look!" Ditoh still whispered with frantic intensity. He pointed at the vertical cliffs that shot up for more than two hundred feet. There were no handholds, no possible way for anyone to get out of the box canyon except by the way the two Apaches had entered.

Both men were silent. *Where had the Belighanna gone?*

"They took him," Alchisay said slowly. "They turned him into one of them."

Ditoh shuddered. Somewhere in that tangle of bones was a new skeleton. The wind whistling overhead was like the moaning of the Mountain Spirits.

Without further talk, the two men turned. Alchisay thought angrily that he had lost a finger and had a mutilated mouth — and all for nothing. True, he had a fine Springfield rifle, but this would be countered by Ditoh's description of the raid. That one would point out that the Mountain Spirits had seen fit to ruin his war party. So, Alchisay reasoned, if he were ever to announce a war party, he would be shunned as someone who had drawn to himself the evil interest of the gods. Proof? Nantije dead, Delchay quitting, a missing finger, a missing lip, no loot, no prisoners — and then, the place of bones.

Ditoh took one backward glance. Then he suddenly

grabbed Alchisay's elbow. Alchisay angrily shook him off. Ditoh wasted no time in arguing. He had seen a living hand was grasping the long lance. Everything suddenly became clear.

But he was not sure; there was too much sorcery in this place. He was a brave man. He turned and walked back toward Slocum. His eyes were fixed on Slocum's hand. As he watched, sweat dripped from under the visor and fell on Slocum's hand.

Just as Ditoh pulled his Colt, Slocum lunged with the lance. Ditoh got off one shot. The bullet struck the cuirass dead center. But by then the lance had gone clean through Ditoh's intestines, snapped the twelfth vertebra and severed the spinal cord.

The impact of the bullet knocked Slocum backwards. It felt as if a vicious mule had kicked him in the chest. But since the cuirass was designed with a ridge running vertically down its front, the bullet was deflected to one side.

Ditoh's legs collapsed. He dropped the Colt and grabbed the lance shaft with both hands and tried to pull it out. Alchisay was paralyzed in astonishment as the knight in armor had moved toward Ditoh. He had not noticed the living hand that held the lance.

Alchisay was sure that the spirit of the dead Spaniard was inside the armor, making it move. He watched, rigid with horror, while Slocum got up, drew the sword, and began to walk toward him.

Alchisay's teeth began to chatter.

Ditoh cried out, "It's the Belighanna!" Alchisay saw that Ditoh was still tugging at the lance. He did not know that it was locked into his spine.

"The Spaniard, the Spaniard! It's the Belighanna!"

Suddenly Alchisay realized what Ditoh was trying to tell him.

He started to raise the Springfield for an aimed shot. The

bullet would have gone through the armor because of its tremendous powder charge. Slocum would have fired from the hip, but Alchisay had never had enough practice.

He was able to snuggle the stock against his cheek when the downstroke hit. It was a heavy blade, designed to cut through just about anything, including light armor. It had cost de Alarcón twenty-four gold ducats in the best sword-smith's in Seville. The razor edge bit into Alchisay's left shoulder, between the neck and the arm socket.

It snapped the shoulder blade as if it were a twig and kept going at a forty-five-degree angle, driven by Slocum's rage. It cut through four ribs as if they were matchsticks, slashed the heart, and finally it came to rest halfway through the sternum. There it lay, jammed by the pressure of the two almost severed parts of that bone.

Alchisay looked down. His left arm, all its nerves and tendons severed, hung inertly by his side. Blood spurted through his chest wall. It was only then that he finally understood that he was not dealing with a ghost. He cradled the Springfield against his stomach and sang his death song while he sank to his knees.

Slocum bent over him and wrenched the Springfield away. There was a strange, yearning look in the Apache's eyes. Slocum knew what it meant: the Chiricahua wanted to be buried with his most precious possession. Slocum never did favors for people who had tortured him. The man would die within seconds. But he could do a favor for the other Apache, who was hitching himself toward him on his elbows, with his knife in his teeth. The lance stuck out grotesquely from his stomach; this forced Ditoh to crawl sideways. The man's labored breathing sounded like a blacksmith's bellows. This was the man who had inserted poisoned spines into Slocum's penis.

Slocum lifted the Springfield and shot him in the heart.

In the few remaining seconds of life that remained to him, Alchisay thought, *If this man had been a Chiricahua, he would have been the greatest one of all.*

14

Slocum stared down into the desert. In the Apache's leather pouch he carried eight cartridges. He had made a sling for the Springfield by cutting up Ditoh's moccasins. The pouch also held a handful of jerky. He had found a *tinaja* that actually held water, and he had drunk his fill. He had filled the canteen the Apaches had previously taken from him.

All in all, he was in good shape.

Then, far out in the blinding white alkali, he saw a tiny figure stumbling and weaving, stumbling, getting up, and walking unsteadily. Then it fell again. It rose, slowly and painfully, and began its erratic movements all over again. At this distance it resembled a crippled ant.

It could only be one person—Wagner.

Slocum angled down from the ridge. He went through the piñons, then through the dwarf oaks. He remembered suddenly that Wagner would very likely be starving. He went back to the piñons, and, with the butt of his Springfield, he banged the branches of the piñons. He filled his pockets to overflowing with the ripe, meaty nuts.

Then he reached the desert floor. Here Wagner was out of sight, but the weaving, erratic track was easy to follow. Here he had tripped over a small *cholla*. Slocum winced when he saw that. Then Wagner had gotten up, braced himself against a *saguaro*, then pushed himself away with an effort. He had continued in his wild, meandering course, but always to the south.

It was impossible to get lost. The skies were always clear. All Wagner had to do was to keep the sun to his left in the morning and to his right in the afternoon. True, occasionally the tracks wobbled to the southwest, and once in a while to the southeast, but the trend was southerly.

"Gotta give 'im credit for *something*," Slocum said aloud.

What Slocum couldn't figure out was where Wagner was getting his water. There were no *tinajas* out here; there were no wells in this part of the Yuma Desert. From his vantage point earlier that morning Slocum had not noticed any barrel cactus in this area. In that heat a man could not last for more than three hours, maybe five at the most, without water. The next step was for him to strip himself naked and run around in circles; that was what men dying of thirst always did.

Yet Wagner was forging ahead.

In twenty minutes Slocum was close enough to Wagner to see that he was not wearing a sombrero. That was the first warning sign that the man was not behaving normally. To move anywhere in the sun without one was an open invitation to sunstroke and final collapse.

When he was fifty feet away he yelled, "Wagner!"

Wagner paid no attention.

Slocum neared. When he was twenty feet in back of the man he tried once more. "Russell!"

Wagner gave no sign that he had heard. Slocum came alongside and said, "Russell." Still there was no response. Slocum felt that something was very wrong indeed. He touched Wagner's elbow while the man kept walking.

Wagner shook it off without even looking at him. He behaved as if Slocum's hand was an irritating fly. He continued with his erratic stumbling. Slocum looked at him closely. Huge water-filled blisters covered the man's scalp. His face was baked brick-red and covered with small blisters. His hands and arms were swollen because of the hundreds of *cholla* and beavertail spines into which he had stumbled. When Wagner licked his cracked, blistered lips, Slocum could see that the swollen, blackening tongue was filled with beavertail spines.

"Wagner," Slocum said gently. He had seen men before who had been driven insane by the desert. Some recovered, some did not. Wagner looked as if he was in the latter group.

Wagner kept walking. Slocum gripped him hard by his right elbow. Wagner came to a stop. He did not turn his head. Slocum thought he was like a patient plow horse whose reins had just been checked.

Slocum held up his canteen and shook it in Wagner's face. Wagner changed expression immediately.

He stared at the canteen for a moment. Then he said something. Slocum could not understand it, because the man's tongue was so swollen. Then he suddenly whimpered and grabbed the canteen. Slocum took it away from him.

"You'll get it," he said. "Relax."

Wagner dropped his swollen hand. Then he sat down as if his legs had been jerked from under him. His face contorted and he began to cry. Slocum unscrewed the canteen. He tore a piece from Wagner's shirt and inserted it into the canteen. When it had soaked up all the water that it could hold, he gave it to Wagner. Wagner began chewing and sucking on it greedily.

This technique permitted a small amount of water at a time to enter his stomach. When he had chewed it dry, Slocum took it from him. As he was dipping it into the canteen again, Wagner made a desperate grab for the canteen. He knocked it from Slocum's hands. By the time Slocum picked it up, half the water had run out onto the desert.

"Asshole!" Slocum said. "Keepin' up the good work, right?"

He soaked the fabric once more and handed it to Wagner. "Keep your distance, you dumb son of a bitch," Slocum said. He was angry. Wagner paid no attention. His mouth sucked and gnawed on the wet rag.

It was fascinating for Slocum to see how the man grew visibly stronger as the water entered his system. In half an hour he had emptied the canteen. His tongue was much smaller.

"How'd you get your mouth full of spines?"

"Wanted somethin' wet. Beavertails was wet."

Slocum looked at him. He had always thought Wagner was stupid; yet how could he criticize a man going crazy from lack of water?

"That doesn't work."

"Yeah. Found out. But I found a source of water," he said, with a triumphant grin. "Somethin' you never thought of, I bet!" He chuckled. "But I'm keepin' *that* a secret. Y' know when you was callin' me back there a ways, know why I din' pay no attention?"

"No, why?"

"'Cause I thought you was a ghost. Yessir, I thought my ol' prison pal was dead. Know when I realized you wasn't?"

"When?" asked Slocum, intrigued in spite of his dislike.

"When I heard the water sloshin' 'roun' in that ol' canteen. I figgered anythin' that sounded so real *was* real— know what I mean?"

"Where's your sombrero?"

"Threw it away. Got too heavy."

"That's pretty smart, Russell." Slocum pulled up Wagner's shirt again and ripped out a sixteen-inch square. He knotted each corner and handed the result to Wagner.

"What the fuck am I gonna do with this?"

Slocum sighed. Wagner was back doing business at the same old stand.

"Put it on your stupid head!" he shouted.

Wagner put it on. "Listen," he said with a grin, "wanna know that source of water?"

"Sure." Slocum handed Wagner two strips of jerky and a handful of piñon nuts. Wagner shook his head. "Don't need it," he said with a broad grin. He handed the food back to Slocum. Then he reached into his pocket and pulled out two half-eaten lizards.

"You been *eatin'* these?"

"Sure. Feelin' disgusted?" There was a weird look in Wagner's eyes.

"Nope. I've eaten grubs from rotten logs."

Wagner looked disappointed. "Well," he said, "that's where I got my water from. Drank their blood. Problem came up. Blood is salty. Found out. Got thirstier than ever."

"Yep," Slocum said. "But a man can't think of everything."

For some reason this struck Wagner as very funny. He

began to laugh. The laughter grew more intense; it edged into hysteria, then he broke down into wild, convulsive sobbing.

That afternoon, Slocum found a grove of barrel cactus. He squeezed the canteen full of water.

They kept going. Wagner did not get any better. He had nightmares. He woke up thrashing and choking, as if he were trying to vomit. He would not let Slocum try to pull the cactus needles from his tongue, which by now had become swollen with pus.

Slocum had tried, but Wagner had bitten his thumb severely. "The hell with it," Slocum said. "Let a doctor take them out when we get to Puerto Peñasco."

Once they saw a rattlesnake sliding away into the mesquite. Wagner turned white and tried to get behind Slocum.

"It's gone," Slocum said soothingly, as if to a child. "It won't hurt you." Wagner trembled.

That night Wagner cried in terror in his sleep. He was convinced that a monster rattler was slowly approaching him with its huge, black forked tongue flicking at him. Slocum had to wake him up. Wagner was afraid to go to sleep again. Slocum guessed that killing and eating the rattlesnakes and lizards had somehow given the man serious guilt feelings, but this was something beyond Slocum's comprehension.

It was a terrible four days for the both of them, what with Wagner's weeping and nightmares, and Slocum's being afraid to take more than a catnap, in case Wagner would take it into his head to kill himself or run into the desert. On the fifth day they staggered into the Posada Carapán.

Mr. Wagner was sitting in the patio drinking a cold limeade. He said coldly, "You're six days late."

A doctor came and extracted the cactus spines from Wagner's tongue with a pair of tweezers. Slocum and two servants had to hold Wagner. He screamed and screamed and a white froth appeared on his lips. It took another two hours to pull the rest of the spines from his legs, arms, and hands. The doctor, Ismael Gomez, painted Wagner's tongue with iodine. Wagner bit Gomez's fingers. The doctor cursed him in fluent, colloquial Spanish. Slocum grinned. Thank God, Russell was now someone else's problem.

He said, in Spanish, "Ask his father for plenty of money. The old man is very rich."

"Ah?"

The doctor spread a soothing salve over the blisters and the sunburn. He said it was the worst case of sunburn he had ever seen. In Spanish, he told Mr. Wagner that the young man needed several days of rest.

"What the hell's the greaser sayin'?" Wagner demanded harshly. The doctor knew what "greaser" meant. He flushed.

"Pregúntele más," Slocum said with a grin. "Ask for more."

The doctor promptly doubled the amount he had been planning to ask. Wagner paid and waited till the doctor left.

Slocum and the elder Wagner looked at Russell. He stood in front of the massive Victorian oak bureau with a bevelled mirror set in back of it. Russell bared his teeth. For a second Slocum thought that he was smiling. Then he gripped the green marble top of the bureau with a hand at each end.

Before they could stop him he had smashed his face into the marble as hard as he could. Several front teeth snapped off. He raised his head for another smash. Slocum was on him with an armlock. He wrestled him away and onto the bed. Russell had broken his nose with the same blow. As the blood bubbled from his mouth and nose, he began chuckling.

"Get the doctor!"

Wagner was frozen.

"Get the goddamn doctor!"

Wagner left. Slocum held Russell flat on the bed. Blood was seeping onto the blanket. He was talking in a weird gibberish. Slocum could not understand what he was saying. Only much later, riding back to Arizona, did he realize that Wagner was punishing his teeth for having bitten into a live rattlesnake, in the hope that the giant rattler that appeared in his dreams would accept this sacrifice and not arrive in his nightmares any more.

Dr. Gomez entered. He gave Russell a sedative. There were, alas, he said, no dentists in Puerto Peñasco. The nearest one was in Guadalajara, far away. Better ones were in Mexico City.

Slocum translated.

"Christ almighty, who wants a greaser dentist!" Wagner exploded, staring at his son's mangled mouth. "I'll take him to San Francisco. What the hell's the matter with you, you no-good bastard?"

Tears oozed from Russell's closed eyes. Then he passed out.

"Little fuck!"

Slocum was sick of the both of them. Wagner turned and started to say something. Slocum held up his hand.

"Pay me," he said softly.

"*Pay* you? You brought me someone who's crazy! He wasn't crazy when he went into Yuma! And you show up six days late! He was all full of blisters. All infected! I don't pay full price for damaged goods, mister!"

Slocum slammed his fist down onto the marble bureau top with such violent ferocity that it cracked across its vertical dimension. He said nothing. He stepped out. He walked down the hall to his room, picked up the Springfield in one hand, one of the huge Springfield cartridges with the other, and walked back.

He kicked open the door. Wagner was standing by his

son's bed with an angry, puzzled expression. Wagner turned. His mouth dropped.

Slocum pulled the bolt back, dropped the cartridge into the chamber, and rammed the bolt forward. The gun was ready to fire. Wagner's son snored away on the bed between the two men.

Wagner's hand went to the butt of his Colt.

"Don't," Slocum said so softly that Wagner could scarcely hear him. Wagner looked into those green eyes. He suddenly remembered why he had hired Slocum in the first place.

Very slowly, he took his hand away. He reached under the bed and pulled out a small leather valise. It was full of twenty-dollar bills.

"Count," Slocum said. "Nice and slow."

When he had finished, Slocum was satisfied. He held out his left hand. Wagner placed the valise in it.

"Now the Colt."

"Look here, Slocum—"

Slocum snapped his fingers. Wagner flushed. For a moment, he toyed with the idea of pretending to hand it over, then making a fast shot. But he saw Slocum's knuckle slowly turn white as it took up the slack on the Springfield trigger.

"Go ahead," Slocum said, almost in a whisper. "It would give me great pleasure."

Wagner sighed and handed over the Colt.

"I don't want you shootin' me in the back from the window when I go by underneath," Slocum said. "No hard feelins?"

Wagner pressed his lips together and was silent.

"I guess there're hard feelins, then," Slocum said, jamming the Colt on top of the money. He did not look regretful.

"I'll leave your Colt with the livery stable," he said. "I'll be buyin' myself a complete new outfit. And a horse an' saddle. I wouldn't come out of the room for about an hour, if I were you. Which I'd certainly hate to be."

"What?" Wagner said, puzzled.

Slocum did not bother to respond. He turned for a last look at Russell Wagner. The blood from the broken nose had coagulated. He was breathing stertorously from his open mouth. The jagged, broken teeth suddenly looked like a rattlesnake's fangs.

The man was probably ruined forever. And there was nothing that anyone could do about it. Especially his father.

"So long, kid," Slocum said, and went out the door.

JAKE LOGAN

___ 0-867-21087	**SLOCUM'S REVENGE**	$1.95
___ 07396-3	**THE JACKSON HOLE TROUBLE**	$2.50
___ 07182-0	**SLOCUM AND THE CATTLE QUEEN**	$2.75
___ 06413-1	**SLOCUM GETS EVEN**	$2.50
___ 06744-0	**SLOCUM AND THE LOST DUTCHMAN MINE**	$2.50
___ 07018-2	**BANDIT GOLD**	$2.50
___ 06846-3	**GUNS OF THE SOUTH PASS**	$2.50
___ 07258-4	**DALLAS MADAM**	$2.50
___ 07139-1	**SOUTH OF THE BORDER**	$2.50
___ 07460-9	**SLOCUM'S CRIME**	$2.50
___ 07567-2	**SLOCUM'S PRIDE**	$2.50
___ 07382-3	**SLOCUM AND THE GUN-RUNNERS**	$2.50
___ 07494-3	**SLOCUM'S WINNING HAND**	$2.50
___ 08382-9	**SLOCUM IN DEADWOOD**	$2.50
___ 07753-5	**THE JOURNEY OF DEATH**	$2.50
___ 07654-7	**SLOCUM'S STAMPEDE**	$2.50
___ 07784-5	**SLOCUM'S GOOD DEED**	$2.50
___ 08101-X	**THE NEVADA SWINDLE**	$2.50
___ 07973-2	**SLOCUM AND THE AVENGING GUN**	$2.50
___ 08031-5	**SLOCUM RIDES ALONE**	$2.50
___ 08087-0	**THE SUNSHINE BASIN WAR**	$2.50
___ 08279-2	**VIGILANTE JUSTICE**	$2.50

Prices may be slightly higher in Canada.

J.D. HARDIN

"THE MOST EXCITING
WESTERN WRITER SINCE
LOUIS L'AMOUR"
—JAKE LOGAN

45